LIMITED
OPTIONS

LIMITED OPTIONS

A Novel

PALMA HARCOURT

BEAUFORT BOOKS
Publishers
New York

Library of Congress Cataloging-in-Publication Data
Harcourt, Palma.
    Limited options.

    I. Title.
PR6058.A62L5   1987   823′.914   87-1055
ISBN 0-8253-0419-9

Published in the United States by Beaufort Books Publishers, New York.

Printed in the U.S.A.   First American Edition 1987

10 9 8 7 6 5 4 3 2 1

Two shots ring out across the Place de l'Opéra in Paris.

The sentence is trite, but the event is trite. Another assassination – or attempted assassination – is taking place, the latest in a wave of such attacks on highly-placed politicians and government officials which is sweeping across Europe. An American Vice-President is murdered during a visit to Bonn; a four-star German General dies in Brussels; the body of the UK Permanent Representative to NATO is shipped back to England from the same city. An historically-minded journalist writes in an English paper that Western leaders are going out all over the Continent, like the lights before World War One.

This time the victim is the President of France, entering the Opéra for a gala performance. In spite of stringent security precautions, a bullet from a high-powered rifle finds its mark. But the President is lucky: the shot is low, and his condition, though grave, is stable.

The authorities reach the conclusion that all these attacks are the work of one man or group. In the past they have been cunning, well-planned and blessed by luck. But in the Place de l'Opéra things are different. The source of the bullet is noted by a sharp-eyed gendarme, and the would-be assassin is forced into hasty flight from his roof-top. He manages to escape, but he is wounded, and his anonymity lost; a television cameraman turns his camera on the police activity and inadvertently gets an excellent picture of the terrorist – a picture that is appearing in the media throughout the Western world.

One

The one-room flat was dreary. Gaps in the uneven floor boards, only partially covered by a thin strip of carpet, revealed the garage below. Patches of damp darkened the wallpaper. Though furniture was minimal – a table, two chairs and a stool, a double bed with squeaky springs, a sleeping-bag in which the girl had spent the night – the general appearance was of clutter. Beside a gas fire, its ceramic elements mostly broken, a kettle was beginning to boil on a noisily spluttering ring.

It was seven-thirty in the morning. Outside it was already a bright, clear day, but little light penetrated the grimy, curtainless windows which fronted on to a narrow London mews. The room smelt of sweat and stale cooking.

There were three people sitting at the table, two men and a girl. They made an incongruous trio.

'For God's sake don't kill the woman. Don't even hurt her badly.'

Trina Hansen spoke harshly and the two men exchanged glances. They accepted that she was in charge, but at the same time they chafed at her authority.

It was almost thirty years since Trina had been christened Katarina Maria Anna in the Russian Church in Ennismore Gardens off Knightsbridge. She was the only child of a German businessman and a White Russian immigrant who claimed to be a countess. The marriage had not been successful, and Trina's parents had separated many years ago, but the German had been generous. Little Trina had wanted for nothing. She enjoyed – or suffered – exclusive schools, expensive holidays abroad, coming-out parties, whatever her mother thought would help to turn her into an English lady.

Trina acquiesced in all this. Indeed, she took advantage of it. She was a clever girl and worked hard; she perfected several languages, acquired a variety of skills, from sailing to ski-ing, and made a large number of suitable friends and acquaintances who were to prove useful later. Subsequently she also made some friends who were much less suitable, and who introduced her to some less usual activities – activities of which neither of her parents would have approved.

When she was eighteen, having refused to go to university, Trina decided to leave her mother's home. Her father was persuaded to buy her a flat off Sloane Square and provide a substantial allowance. She spent a lot of time abroad, but took care to keep her English connections. She was twenty when she met Horst Zabel and began what was to prove a lasting relationship. Zabel was the one person – man or woman – whom Trina respected and admired; it was trite, she knew, especially in the circles in which they moved, but she would do – and had done – anything for him. The present operation was just one example.

'You suggesting I'm a duff driver?' Bruno Dieke said resentfully, with a heavy frown. He was a big, strong man, and he wore dirty dungarees over an old T-shirt.

Unexpectedly the second man – Frank Roth – shifted his skinny buttocks on the hard stool and reached across the table to ruffle Dieke's fair, almost white, hair. Roth was dark-haired, whey-faced. Twenty-three years old – ten years younger than Dieke – he had the air of a helpless orphan; in fact his most valuable asset was his street-wise cunning. He too wore soiled workmen's overalls, but on him they looked somehow incongruous, contrasting as they did with his soft, white hands. If Dieke was the brawn of the partnership, Roth was the brains.

'You'll take care, won't you, Bruno,' he said appeasingly.

'You'd better,' said the girl. 'If anything goes wrong and

8

the Linton woman gets hers, the fuzz'll be after you, and they won't let it rest. I told you her husband's in the Home Office, and he's got influence – real influence. So you'd better obey orders and see she stays safe.'

The kettle boiled and Roth got up to make the tea. Dieke returned to cutting the loaf. There was butter and jam on the table, their breakfast.

'She'll be fine, Trina. Shaken a bit, maybe, but no more. I know my business.' Dieke was sullen. 'You've no cause to worry.'

Trina nodded and smiled grimly, taking the piece of bread he passed her. This was no time to quarrel. Inevitably the three of them were tense and edgy before an operation, however experienced they might be. She began to eat.

'More tea, Trina?' Roth asked.

Trina looked at her watch. They had to be there at exactly the right time, too early and they might be noticed, too late and they would miss the car. 'Why not?' she said and pushed her mug towards the pot.

Roth poured. Dieke was fumbling in his pocket and Trina looked up sharply as he brought out a small, battered rectangular tin. She shook her head impatiently.

'Not now, Bruno.'

'Why not? One joint's not going to hurt.'

'It's her gear,' Roth said, laughing. 'She's got up to look like a schoolmarm, so she's acting like one.'

Dieke put a joint in his mouth and lit a match. Immediately Trina sprang up from the table and moved to the furthest corner of the room. She controlled her temper.

'Don't light it, Bruno! Frank's right. It *is* my gear.' She was wearing a neat grey suit, with a pink blouse, beige stockings and flat brown shoes. The intended impression was of careful, sensible buying on a limited budget. Her voice level, she continued, 'Do you imagine the woman's going to trust me if I stink of cannabis? I'm meant to be a respectable, responsible character. Anyway, I don't want you high. Cut it out till afterwards.'

'Sure, Trina. Sorry.' Dieke blew out the match, replaced the joint in its tin and pushed the tin away from him. 'Okay. I'll save it for later.'

In spite of the seemingly ready apology, Trina was aware of Bruno Dieke's suppressed anger at her rebuke, an anger shared by Roth. She was suddenly thankful that she had taken every precaution to conceal her true identity from the two men; she didn't wholly trust either of them. But then there were very few people whom she trusted absolutely; it was how she had managed to stay alive and keep out of prison for so long.

'It's time we started to get ready,' she said at length.

The men began to tidy the room. Roth cleared away the breakfast. Dieke hastily pulled the bed together and rolled up the sleeping-bag. They didn't take much care with their chores. The two of them would be returning later.

Trina had gone to the bathroom. A rusty tub with a high water mark furred with dirt, broken tiles, a leaky cistern, an unspeakable lavatory pan. Her nose wrinkled with disgust. On the other hand the light in here was adequate and the mirror on the wall – an advertising give-away, the name of the advertiser spelt out round the edge – wasn't cracked. She could see what she was doing.

From a small hold-all Trina took a cosmetic case and a wig. Carefully she made up her face, disguising her high Slavonic cheekbones, flattening her nose. With plumpers in her cheeks, the silver-grey wig hiding her blonde hair and a pair of unfashionable thin-rimmed spectacles, she had added more than a dozen years to her age. She regarded herself with satisfaction.

Taking a plain gold ring from her jacket pocket she slipped it on to the third finger of her left hand. 'Hello, Mrs Carpenter,' she said, and laughed softly; it was the name of a friend of her mother's whom she disliked.

Frank Roth clapped twice in mock applause as she

returned to the room. 'Look, Bruno! Isn't she great?'

'Great!' Dieke agreed after a moment's hesitation. Almost against his will he nodded his approval. 'Your own mother wouldn't recognize you, Trina.'

'I hope not,' Trina said shortly. 'If we're all set, let's go.'

The three of them left the flat and went down rickety stairs to the garage below. Dieke turned on the light and the naked bulb revealed a red Ford Escort, two years old, a small dent in the rear but otherwise immaculate. Trina had borrowed it from an accommodating friend, and Dieke had fitted false number plates the night before. There were hundreds of similar cars being driven around London every day.

The other vehicle was a white van, dirty and nondescript. Roth had stolen it earlier that morning. It belonged to a man who worked nights, so it was unlikely to be missed for some hours. By that time, if all went well, they would have abandoned it.

Roth opened the garage doors and made sure the mews was empty before waving Trina out. As soon as she had bumped over the cobbles and turned into the street, he motioned to Dieke to follow. Then he closed and locked the garage, before hopping into the passenger's seat of the van. The small convoy was ready.

Dieke, who had pocketed his tin of joints while Trina was in the bathroom, lit two and passed one to Roth. 'Your cap,' Roth reminded him, and Dieke pulled a painter's cap over his too easily identifiable fair hair.

They grinned at each other. 'Hampstead, here we come,' Dieke said, starting the engine, and Roth slapped him on the thigh in return. At that moment they could have been any young men on their way to an ordinary day's work. There was nothing in their appearance to suggest menace.

★

'Eat up your breakfast, Derek dear.' Julia Linton – a pretty woman, fair-haired, brown-eyed, now approaching middle age – put another slice of bread in the toaster, and smiled from her nephew to her husband.

Geoffrey Linton returned her smile, and together they watched the boy pushing his scrambled egg around his plate. Normally Derek Maidment's plate would have been clean long before this, but today was special. They accepted this and were prepared to be indulgent, ready to yield to their ever-present temptation to spoil him.

Linton glanced at his watch. 'You've plenty of time, Julia, but I'd better be off.' He dropped his napkin on to the table, pushed back his chair and stood. A tall, thin man in his late forties, hair greying, shoulders a little stooped, he could have been taken for a doctor or a lawyer or almost any professional man. In fact, he was a civil servant, and considered to be one of the best brains in the Home Office. He regarded his nephew half seriously, half humorously. 'So I'll say goodbye, Derek. Have a good holiday. Don't break a leg on the ski slopes, and we'll see you after Easter.'

'Yes, Uncle. Thank you, Uncle.'

The boy, small for his nearly ten years, slid to his feet and solemnly offered his hand. Geoffrey Linton shook it with equal solemnity. To hide her amusement, Julia busied herself with the toaster. Six months ago Derek would have held up his face to be kissed, but boarding school had changed all that. She wasn't surprised, just a little saddened, remembering in a moment of nostalgia her own sons, now both grown men, at Derek's age. She followed her husband into the hall.

Linton slipped on a raincoat and picked up his briefcase. 'I've a busy day ahead, darling. I'll probably be late, but I'll phone.'

'Right. We're not doing –'

Julia stopped, making a grimace as the roar of a vacuum cleaner, accompanied by loud off-key singing, put an end to their conversation. Mrs Walker, who came in to help three mornings a week, had started work. Geoffrey bent and kissed his wife goodbye.

'Take care,' he mouthed.

'Take care yourself,' she replied.

It was their private formula whenever they parted from each other. Geoffrey let himself out of the house and opened the big double garage which held his Jaguar and Julia's Renault. He drove off, leaving the garage door conveniently open for her, and turned left, past the church, towards the distant main road. Except that he had to draw out to avoid it, he paid no attention to the red Ford Escort parked a little way along the quiet street of large, detached houses.

Trina Hansen drew a deep breath and slowly blew it out as she saw the Jaguar turn the corner and disappear. Things were going well, so far. Though traffic had been excessively heavy, the journey from the mews to Hampstead had taken no longer than had been estimated. She had arrived within minutes of the planned moment, to find the white van already in position on the side road, which entered the Lintons' street from the right some twenty-five yards ahead, forming a small T-junction opposite a large church in a broad churchyard.

Anyway, Geoffrey Linton had gone. During the week, which was all she had had to do the necessary research, she had learnt that he didn't leave the house at a precise time each day. His departure could vary by anything up to three-quarters of an hour and she had feared that today he might be late, might even leave simultaneously with his wife. Luckily he hadn't. Another variable factor had turned in their favour. But they were still only at the start of the operation.

Trina could feel her tension mounting. She kept her eyes fixed on her rear-view mirror, in which she could see the entrance to the Lintons' driveway. It wouldn't be much longer. Julia Linton couldn't risk being late at Heathrow, so that the boy missed his flight. Julia would allow for traffic hold-ups, parking, handing over the boy to the care of the Swissair hostess, and for any unexpected eventuality that might delay her.

Impatiently Trina shifted in her seat and looked at the car clock; surely the wretched woman must appear soon. Then in the distance behind her, she saw a milk float turn into the road, and she swore under her breath. The float could mean trouble. The houses here were all widely-spaced; there wouldn't be many deliveries to make, and if the milkman's arrival at the junction coincided with the Linton woman in her Renault . . . She wished she could warn Bruno Dieke, who wouldn't be able to see the possibility from where he was parked, but they hadn't thought it worth bothering with CB radios or walkie-talkies or complications of that kind.

Gritting her teeth, Trina Hansen watched as the milk float came inexorably closer. Still the Renault didn't drive out.

*

Had Trina but known it, her impatience was shared by young Derek Maidment. Hopping from one foot to another, he willed his aunt to put down the telephone. It had rung just as they were about to leave the house. She could have ignored it, but no. Not only had she answered it, but she was yakking away as if time was of no importance, as if no plane was waiting. Angrily Derek kicked at his bag, abandoned inside the front door.

Julia looked up. She was smiling and nodding. 'Yes,' she said. 'We shall be delighted. Thank you very much.' She listened for a moment. 'You'll be sending us a "*pour mémoire*"? Good. Thank you again.'

She put down the receiver, and immediately dialled another number. Derek, who had been about to pick up his bag, groaned aloud. 'Aunt Julia!' he protested.

'Won't be a minute, Derek.'

Biting his lip, the small boy turned away. What would happen if he missed the plane? Was there a flight later? Would he be able to get a seat? And what about Dad? Would Dad wait for him at the airport? How would Dad know when he was coming if he wasn't on the right plane? Surely no phone call was so important that . . .

'Yes,' Julia Linton was saying. 'Wednesday week. Dinner at Number Ten. The PM's social secretary just phoned. Tell Mr Linton when he gets in, will you?' She replaced the receiver, and called up the stairs. 'We're going now, Mrs Walker. I'll be back before you leave.'

'Very good, Madam.'

Julia picked up Derek's bag. 'Come along, dear,' she said.

It was an unnecessary remark. Derek had already opened the front door and was expectantly waiting for his aunt. When she followed him he almost danced down the steps on to the gravel drive. Minutes later he was ensconced in the back seat of the Renault, his seat belt fastened, his bag beside him. His face was bright with anticipation as they edged through the gates on to the road.

Two

'There's the Escort!' said Frank Roth, a sudden tightening of the voice his only sign of emotion.

He plucked the joint from Bruno Dieke's mouth as Dieke started the engine, and ground it out on the floor of the van. By now the atmosphere in the cab was thick with the sickly sweet smell of cannabis. Dieke was used to the stuff, and showed no signs of a 'high' that might impede the operation; nevertheless, Roth would have preferred to drive himself, though he dared not suggest it; driving was Dieke's job.

Dieke moved the van a few yards forward to the T-junction and glanced quickly from side to side, ready to let in the clutch and accelerate at the right moment. A short distance away in one direction, Trina's red Escort, which moments ago had gone past the end of the side road – the pre-arranged signal – was parked again. In the other direction, in the middle of the block, a milkman was loading dairy produce from his vehicle into a plastic basket: his deliveries were taking longer than usual this morning. And, about to cross the road junction, and thus pass immediately in front of them, was Julia Linton in her Renault, the Maidment boy sitting in the rear seat.

The situation was ideal, no pedestrians or other moving vehicles were in sight, and the milk float was too far away to cause a problem. With a broad grin of satisfaction, Dieke drove directly at the side of the Renault. His orders were to hit the car with sufficient force to immobilize it, but not to cause excessive damage, and then to drive straight on. It was to be an unimportant accident, a stolen van, a hit-and-run driver, but no one seriously hurt – nothing to give the police cause for undue worry. There were too many such minor incidents in London each week. The whole thing should have been child's play for Dieke.

And it nearly was. His timing was perfect, but his judgement of speed – impaired perhaps by cannabis – was poor.

Julia had no chance. She had been an excellent driver ever since she could legally hold a licence. Her reactions were quick, and she was careful. She saw the van seconds before it hurtled towards her, but evasive action was impossible.

There was a loud thud, followed by the sound of tearing metal and breaking glass as the van hit the Renault, lifting it across the pavement and pinioning it against the wall of the churchyard opposite. Derek screamed. Julia felt an excruciating pain in her side that seemed to travel down her leg; then everything went black.

'Christ! You've done it now, mate,' Frank Roth said.

Dieke was trying to restart his stalled engine, but the task was hopeless. The front of the van had crumpled in the collision, and there was an ominous noise of water trickling from its radiator. He swore violently, again trying the starter without response. He began to sweat.

Roth took charge. 'Bruno! Come on, man! Let's get out of here! This heap's not going to move.' He had the door open and was about to jump down. Almost reluctantly Dieke prepared to follow. The van had promised a safe get-away. Now it was useless. Trina had left her car and was already running back to the scene. Instinctively the two men turned in the opposite direction.

Derek was shocked but, apart from a bruise or two, unharmed. He freed himself from his safety-belt and, leaning over the front seat, shook Julia by the shoulder. 'Auntie! Aunt Julia, are you all right? Aunt Julia!'

Julia Linton, conscious that someone was calling her name, made a great effort to swim up out of the dark sea in which she was drowning. As she surfaced she became aware of her surroundings, and a high, frightened voice speaking to her, demanding to know if she was all right. Derek!

The present returned to her in a rush. She struggled to sit up, but found she couldn't move without causing herself extreme pain down the right side of her body.

'I seem to have hurt myself a little, darling, but I don't expect it's serious,' she said levelly, doubting that she spoke the truth. 'What about you?'

'I'm okay. I bruised my funny bone. That's all.'

'Oh dear!' Julia bit her lip until she tasted blood. She must not lose consciousness again, not yet, not before help came, she told herself desperately. There was a strong smell of petrol in the car. If it caught fire . . . She turned her head as far as she could, and forced herself to speak calmly. 'Derek, see if you can open the door. If you can, get out of the car. Quickly, dear.'

Derek pushed himself across the seat and was struggling to open the door when it was opened for him from the outside. A lady in a grey suit and pink blouse helped him to climb out, then reached in to get his bag which had fallen on to the floor in the collision and was wedged behind the driver's seat.

'You poor dears,' Trina Hansen said breathlessly. 'Are you all right? No, I can see you're not. That wicked man. He came straight out of that side street and hit you – He must have been drunk, driving like that.'

Trina glanced hurriedly up and down the road. There was no sign of Dieke or Roth, and the van had been abandoned, crushed at right angles into the offside of the Renault. Inwardly she cursed the two men, but she had no time to bother with them now. The milkman had dropped his basket and was hurrying towards her. A car had drawn up some twenty yards further back and its driver was getting out. Soon there would be more people. There was probably no one in the church to hear, but the crash might well have been noticed in the houses on the corners of the side road opposite, though they were set well back from the road. Time was short.

She leaned over towards Julia. 'I don't think I should move if I were you,' she said. 'Best not to try. Not till the ambulance gets here. They'll know what to do. You'll be fine in hospital,' she added reassuringly.

'Thank you,' Julia murmured. She closed her eyes. She was having great difficulty in concentrating. She kept feeling as if she were about to drift away down a long dark tunnel, but she knew there was something she must deal with first. 'Derek,' she said. 'The boy. Heathrow. . . He was to catch a flight. . . His father expects him. . . Phone, please . . . my husband.'

'Of course,' Trina said. 'I understand. I'll drive him to the airport and make sure he gets his plane. At least I can do that for you. He's got his ticket?'

'Yes . . . Yes . . . But – '

'Don't worry.'

By now the milkman was at Trina's elbow. 'I saw it all,' he said. 'Hit and run, that's what it was. The two chaps from the van, they've made off. I thought of chasing them, but they were too quick for me. Anyway, I couldn't have stopped them.' He was an elderly man, on the verge of retirement and he spoke defensively, afraid he might be accused of a lack of courage. He peered past Trina into the Renault. 'It's Mrs Linton. Three houses down. I deliver her milk. How is she? Not dead, is she?'

'Certainly not. But she may be badly hurt. We must get help for her.'

Trina looked up as the driver of the car that had stopped reached them. She had hoped it would be someone unsure what to do, easy to manipulate, not too observant, but it was a man in army uniform, a major, who at once made it clear that he intended to take charge of the situation.

He looked quickly at Julia Linton and spoke immediately. 'Ambulance, police been phoned? No? Why not? Oh well, I'll do it. You two stay here, but don't touch her.'

'Yes, sir,' the milkman said, obediently accepting authority.

Trina, however, had no intention of waiting for anyone, and certainly not for the police. She had already delayed too long, though in fact only minutes had elapsed since the crash. As soon as the major had disappeared into the driveway of the nearest house, she picked up Derek's bag. 'We can't wait,' she said to the milkman. 'We've a plane to catch. The little boy has to go to Geneva. Come on, Derek dear. Your auntie wants me to take you to Heathrow.'

'No!' Derek said firmly. 'I can't leave her, not like this.'

Trina forced herself to smile. She bent down towards the boy. She hadn't liked the look of that army type; she could imagine him raising difficulties, demanding that she remain as a witness, trying to prevent her taking the boy – by physical force, if necessary.

'Derek, the ambulance will be here very soon, but if we delay you'll miss your flight, and what'll your father do if you don't arrive? He won't know what's happened and he'll be terribly worried. This milkman knows where your aunt lives, and he and the officer'll look after her and get in touch with your uncle.'

'Yes, but – '

'Your aunt *wants* you to go with me, dear. You ask her and she'll tell you.'

Trina was suggesting the impossible. One glance into the Renault was enough for Derek to realize that Aunt Julia was incapable of telling him anything. Face white, eyes shut, breathing heavily, she had lapsed once more into unconsciousness. He had to decide for himself.

Every instinct, every warning against strangers, told him he should stay with his aunt, and not go with this woman whom he'd never seen before. But – but perhaps this was different. Aunt Julia must have explained, must have asked the woman to take him to Heathrow, else she wouldn't have known that he was on his way to Geneva and that Dad would be waiting to meet him there. It must be all right.

As he hesitated, the milkman said, 'Off you go then, sonny, and don't worry about your auntie. Like the lady says, we'll sort things out, me and the army gentleman what's gone to phone.'

It was the encouragement that Derek needed. He smiled doubtfully at the milkman, whom he knew by sight, cast one last look at Julia, and obediently went with Trina Hansen as she hurried him away. When he got to Geneva, he assured himself, he would tell Dad all about it. Dad would know what to do. He could phone from Switzerland and speak to Uncle Geoffrey and find out how Aunt Julia was. Surely everything would be all right; Aunt Julia couldn't be badly hurt. In spite of himself, Derek's spirits began to rise.

★

At the moment of the crash Mrs Walker had just finished cleaning Derek's room – the room he always occupied when he stayed with the Lintons. She heard a dull thud in the distance and the distinctive tinkle of falling glass, and tut-tutted to herself. People drove too fast, people were careless, no wonder there were so many accidents, she thought dismissively. It never occurred to her to associate the frightening sounds with Julia Linton and, unconcerned, Mrs Walker continued with her work.

She unplugged the vacuum cleaner, coiled up its lead and pushed the machine on to the landing. Returning to the room she looked around. Everything was neat and tidy as it should be, the bed newly made, ready for young Derek to spend a couple of nights when he returned from visiting his father and before going back to boarding school. She shook her head sadly. She felt sorry for the boy, his mother dead, his father abroad, no brothers or sisters. The Lintons did their best, but it wasn't the right sort of life for a child, not in her opinion.

Mrs Walker's philosophizing came to an abrupt end as she heard footsteps pounding down the public path that ran between the Lintons' house and the next property. There was an urgency about the running steps that momentarily alarmed her, and she hurried to the window and looked down. From this height she could see over the fence that shielded the path.

In fact, there was nothing really alarming to be seen, merely two workmen, house painters perhaps. One of them was wearing a cotton cap with a big peak, the kind that painters often wore to keep drips off their heads. The cap fell off as he ran, and Mrs Walker saw that his hair was fair, almost white. She watched with diminishing interest as they both disappeared into the distance. There seemed no reason for their violent haste; no one was pursuing them that she could see. People were funny.

Shrugging her incomprehension, Mrs Walker returned to her chores and the two men, Frank Roth and Bruno Dieke, approaching the end of the footpath, slowed as if reaching the edge of a cliff. Ahead lay a road of somewhat smaller houses, but a busier road than the one where the Lintons lived, more people about, more traffic, even a solitary shop masquerading as an art gallery.

'Quick!' Roth said. 'Strip your overalls and reverse your T-shirt.'

He was already doing what he urged. Now, in tight jeans, their appearance was changed. Dieke's hair was still a giveaway if anyone had noticed it, but nothing could be done about that. Roth rolled the two pairs of overalls into a compact bundle and stuffed it under his arm.

'Come on,' he ordered. 'Walk, Bruno. Not too fast, but like we knew where we were going. And keep your eyes skinned. We need wheels. Nothing fancy, though we can't be too choosy.'

Within minutes they found what they were seeking. A woman in a blue Metro drew up a few yards ahead of them, plucked a parcel from the seat beside her and, not bothering to lock the car, ran up a short driveway and rang a doorbell. When the door opened, she stood on the step, absorbed in her conversation, oblivious of what was happening in the road behind her.

The two men wasted no time. Without being told Dieke positioned himself to conceal Roth as the latter gently opened the offside door and slid behind the wheel; as he expected, the key was in the ignition. The moment Dieke heard the engine start he swung himself in beside Roth.

'A gift! A gift!' Roth laughed with satisfaction as the Metro gathered speed. 'The stupid bitch! She was asking for it to be nicked.'

Dieke who had been looking out of the rear window to make sure they were not being followed, relaxed in his seat. He lit his last joint, took a puff and passed it to Roth. 'So it's all turned out okay in the end,' he said, stretching his legs comfortably in front of him.

'It may. If our luck holds.' Roth was suddenly sober. 'The van doesn't matter, but remember what Trina said about Linton having pull. If you did waste his old woman, the fuzz'll be bursting their guts out to find us.'

★

The red Ford Escort was heading along the M4 Motorway towards Heathrow. Trina Hansen drove at a steady pace. Traffic was moderately heavy, but there had been no hold-ups on either of the narrow overpasses. She had given up any attempt at conversation with her passenger; if he didn't want to talk it was all right with her. She was happy to drive and think of Horst Zabel and how pleased he'd be to know that the first stage of the operation had been successful.

It hadn't been perfectly executed, of course, thanks to that fool Dieke, but with any luck Julia Linton hadn't been seriously hurt, so that the police shouldn't be overly curious.

In any case, Roth and Dieke had clearly got away, and the Linton woman was unlikely to cause trouble. If she hadn't actually given her consent for 'Mrs Carpenter' to take her nephew to the airport, she would probably imagine in her semi-conscious state that she had – especially when she heard that the boy had arrived safely in Geneva.

Trina glanced over her shoulder at Derek Maidment, the object of the exercise. He sat huddled in a corner of the back seat, obviously not happy, but accepting the situation.

Indeed, Derek was even less happy than he appeared. He had sensed a change in this strange woman who said her name was Mrs Carpenter. Once they were in her car, and speeding away from Aunt Julia – poor Aunt Julia – she had become much more, much more . . . Derek searched for words that would describe Mrs Carpenter's new, different self. Fierce? Bullying? No, those were too strong. But uncaring, brusque, determined? She reminded him of the matron at his school, whom he disliked because he was afraid of her, though he wouldn't have admitted his fear.

Still, this Mrs Carpenter was taking him to Heathrow, and before long he would be in the air and on his way. Every minute or two he checked his Swiss watch, a present from his father on his last birthday. In spite of all that had happened since they left the house they weren't late. He had plenty of time to catch his flight, and they were getting along well. The road signs, indicating the route to the airport at regular intervals, were reassuring. They would soon be there, and then a Swissair hostess would take charge of him. Not that he really needed her – he was used to travelling to Switzerland; he even knew what the airline staff called him: a 'UM' for 'Unaccompanied Minor', and he didn't think much of the name. Nevertheless, on this occasion a hostess might be useful; at least she would cope with Mrs Carpenter.

Suddenly he sat up straight. They should have been keeping to the left here, ready to turn on to the airport slip road, but instead they were moving over into the right lane.

He didn't understand. The directions were clearly marked. He leant forward and touched Trina on the shoulder.

'Mrs Carpenter, we're going the wrong way.'

'No, we're not, Derek. I know what I'm doing.'

'But we are. This isn't the way to the airport and you promised to take me. I'll miss my plane.'

'We're going to visit a friend of mine.'

'No, no. I don't want to. I want to go to Heathrow. I must. I've got to catch my plane. Dad'll be waiting for me.'

'Derek, it's not what *you* want. It's what *I* want. Now, be quiet and stop breathing down my neck.'

Derek had sounded tearful and frightened, but Trina didn't bother to reassure him. It was a pity he'd been so quick to realize they weren't going to the airport but, since he had, she saw no point in trying to deceive him. Let him cry, she thought; he'd have more to cry about soon.

But at first Derek didn't cry; anger and frustration kept tears at bay. As hard as he could, he began to bang Trina on the shoulder. 'Take me back! Take me back!' he shouted. His fingers gripped her hair and he pulled, wanting to hurt her. To his horror, her hair came away in his hand, and he was falling backwards when she half turned and clouted him on the side of the head.

He lay on the floor of the car, stunned by the blow. His face hurt, and his mind was a blur of unhappiness. It was worse than when his mother had died because then he hadn't been alone. Dad had been with him and they had comforted each other. Now Dad was far away. Perhaps he'd never see him again. Perhaps this dreadful woman was taking him somewhere to kill him, and Dad would never know what had happened.

Then the tears came, and Derek wept. Trina felt no pity for him. She drove on, reminding herself to warn Nana Smith that a close watch must be kept on the boy, that he was cleverer than he looked, that he could turn nasty unexpectedly.

Three

Rory Maidment arrived at Cointrin very early. Geneva's airport was only some fifteen minutes' drive from the British Consulate on the Rue de Vermont where he worked and, as usual when he was meeting Derek, he had allowed himself far too much time. But on one occasion he had been held up at the office and Derek had been forced to wait; he wouldn't forget the look of unadulterated joy on the young face when the boy at last caught sight of him. He had sworn he would never be late again.

Today, however, his anxiety had really been exaggerated. Silently he laughed at himself. He knew that his love for his son – his tendency to spoil him – bordered on the obsessive; it was something he fought against. He wandered around the boutiques, his lanky figure showing no signs of a civil servant's sedentary life. Tall, fair-haired and brown-eyed, he was bronzed from ski-ing in the winter sunshine. And the lines of sadness in his face, which made him look older than he was, somehow added to his attractiveness. It was four years since Sarah, Derek's mother, had died in childbirth, their daughter stillborn, and only recently had his grief ceased to haunt him.

His thoughts turned, as nowadays they often did, to Marie-Louise Grandin. If Derek liked her, if they took to each other . . . He grinned wryly as he resisted the temptation to buy Derek yet another present for his approaching tenth birthday. Instead he bought himself an English paper at the news-stand, and settled down with an espresso at a café table.

The paper didn't make original reading. There were the usual wars and rumours of wars, details of atrocities, political charges and counter-charges, disarmament talks that everyone knew would fail, famine in Africa, floods in Pakistan, coups, assassinations. Maidment looked around him. Maybe the recent attack on the French President accounted for the obviously increased police activity at Cointrin this morning, though luckily this shouldn't affect a direct flight from London.

Maidment shrugged his shoulders and put down his paper. It was Derek who mattered. Christmas had been something of a disaster, with the boy catching measles, and to make up for it he was determined that this holiday should be particularly memorable. Apart from visiting Marie-Louise, they would . . .

Here his thoughts were interrupted by a metallic voice from the public address system: 'Swissair announce the arrival of their Flight SR 831 from London.'

The announcement was made first in French, but Rory Maidment didn't wait for the other languages to follow. He gulped the rest of his coffee, thrust the newspaper into his briefcase and hurried to the Arrivals Hall. He was unaware that he was being watched.

Arndt Gunther smiled with satisfaction as Maidment pushed his way to the front of those crowding around the barrier, so that Derek would see him as soon as the boy was brought through by the air hostess. The passengers from the London flight began to arrive, a trickle, then a stream, a pause, then more.

Maidment was quite aware of the procedure with unaccompanied children. They were usually asked to wait until everyone else had left the aircraft before disembarking, so Derek was apt to appear among the last.

Gunther took the letter from the pocket of his windbreaker. He wanted Maidment to sweat a little, but not enough to commence inquiries. He needed to judge the

27

perfect moment. As he saw Maidment frown and look about him, he sensed that the man had begun to worry.

'*Porteur!*'

'*Monsieur?*'

'You see that *type* over by the barrier? Dark grey business suit and a briefcase. Give him this letter, will you?'

'*Oui, monsieur. C'est tout?*'

'That's all.'

Gunther grinned as he handed over a carefully-judged tip. His wasn't a memorable face, and he was sure the porter would never be able to identify him again with any certainty. The man would probably have forgotten the routine errand in a couple of hours. Gunther walked away, then turned to watch from a distance as Maidment tore open the envelope.

Rory Maidment let the unaddressed envelope fall to the ground, and stood quite still, staring at the handwritten note inside it:

'If you hope to see your son Derek alive again, go straight home and wait for a telephone call. DO NOT INFORM ANYONE THAT HE HAS NOT ARRIVED.'

The second sentence was in block capitals. Maidment crumpled the note in his fist. It was unbelievable. It couldn't be true. No one would want to kidnap Derek. What the hell would there be to gain? He – Maidment – was neither rich nor influential. He was merely a British Consul in Geneva, not even the Consul-General. No, it must be a joke. Someone with a sick sense of humour, who knew how much Derek meant to him, had sent this stupid message. But who – who could do such a thing? Who could hate him so much?

Seconds later Maidment's initial anger gave way to fear. Derek had clearly not arrived on the planned flight. His instinct was to go to the Inquiry Desk and demand some action – a look at the manifest, a call to London. It was the feel of the paper in his clenched fist that stopped him. Whoever wrote it must have known – in advance – that the boy would not arrive. There was no way it could be a hoax.

He smoothed out the note and re-read it. People moved around him. A porter with a baggage trolley asked him to get out of the way, and he did so automatically. A woman knocked against him and apologized, but he paid her no attention. For a minute he was unaware of his surroundings, his mind stilled with shock.

Then, as his brain began to function again, he realized he must move. If the note meant anything at all, it was quite likely that his reactions were under observation. The main thing was to do – or appear to do – as he'd been told. He hurried from the terminal to his car. He would drive home, and – what? Wait for the promised phone call? Perhaps. Or get hold of Julia, who should have taken Derek to Heathrow, and Geoffrey. Could the plan be to put pressure on Geoffrey via Derek and himself? Far-fetched, perhaps, but not impossible.

Thankful that he was beginning to think rationally, Maidment realized with horror that he was accepting the contents of the note as valid. Unwillingly but inevitably, his reason was telling him that unless he acted in accordance with his instructions, Derek might be – would be – killed.

*

It took Maidment more than half an hour to reach the house he rented across the Rhône, not far from the Cathedral of Saint Pierre. Most of the foreign community chose to live in elegant villas along the shores of Lac Léman, or in one of the many luxury apartment blocks that had sprung up to the north of the city, beyond the Place des Nations and the old League of Nations building that now housed the European offices of the United Nations and was the site for an apparently unending series of international conferences. Maidment preferred the twisting streets and village-like atmosphere of Geneva's old town.

When the chance came to sublet 5, Rue de Haut, from a

university professor who had been offered a two-year stint at Harvard, he had jumped at it. The place was too big for him and too expensive, but Derek loved it – the uneven floors, the old beams, the low ceilings, the many rooms, the two staircases, the cobbled courtyard. It had been modernized, with extra bathrooms and a more than adequate kitchen, and Maidment considered it well worth the money.

He turned carefully into the stone archway, for the car was a tight fit. As a British official – a consular officer with the equivalent of diplomatic status – Maidment had to drive a British car, and with his diplomatic discount he had been able to afford a Jaguar, which he had chosen for its power, useful on the long continental Autoroutes. He didn't bother to garage the car, but left it in the courtyard of the house and hurried to let himself into the hall – an extension of the main salon. He had reached a decision: he must phone Geoffrey Linton. Geoffrey was the best man to help him deal with the situation – if indeed there *was* a situation; in spite of his rational conviction, part of his brain still refused to believe it.

The telephone was on a table under the curve of the stairs, and it rang as he was putting his hand out towards it. He snatched up the receiver. 'Rory Maidment here.'

'Ah, Mr Maidment. Good. You received my message about your son, Derek?'

It was a man's voice. He spoke in English, but his English was accented – either German or Dutch, Maidment surmised – and he sounded young, businesslike and aggressive. This was no kind of joke.

Maidment swallowed the bile that rose suddenly in his throat.

'Yes. Where's Derek? What the hell have you done with him?'

'Please, Mr Maidment, keep calm. I'll ask the questions,' said Arndt Gunther quietly and firmly. 'You listen. First, have you attempted to contact anyone about my message? Have you told anyone that Derek has been – er – removed from his family's loving care?'

'No! Not yet. But, by God, if anything happens to him I'll – '

'Nothing will happen to him, Mr Maidment, not if you do as you're told. You understand?'

'I understand what you're saying.' Maidment was recovering some element of composure.

'Fine. Now, try to understand this.' The voice had become cold and incisive. 'This morning a car accident was engineered in Hampstead, when your sister was starting out to take Derek to Heathrow. A lady, a Mrs Carpenter, stopped to help. She promised to take Derek to the airport. In fact, she delivered him to a house in the country.'

'But why? Why?'

'We need him as a hostage for your good behaviour, Mr Maidment.'

'*My* good behaviour? You must be crazy. I don't know who you are, but I'm damn sure there's nothing I can do for you.'

'That's where you're wrong, Mr Maidment, though for the moment we shall ask little of you. Your immediate instructions are these, Mr Maidment, and they are quite simple. You are to telephone and inquire after your sister. You are to say that Mrs Carpenter delivered Derek safely to Heathrow, and he has arrived in Geneva. He was a little shaken by the accident, but otherwise he's fine. However, to your friends and acquaintances in Switzerland, Mr Maidment, you are to tell a different story. You will say that the boy has mumps, and will not be able to spend Easter with you.'

Gunther paused to emphasize what he was about to add.

'Mr Maidment, the essential point is that no one, absolutely no one other than ourselves, should know that there is any cause for concern over Derek. Remember, Mr Maidment – ' Rory found the constant repetition of his name increasingly unbearable ' – that very unpleasant things can happen to small boys. But I repeat, do not worry. He will be all right as long as you do as I say.'

'How – how do I know he's not already dead?' Maidment almost choked on the words.

'Mr Maidment, you do not. But we will let you speak with him in a day or two if it will make you happy.'

'Happy!'

'Now, Mr Maidment, remain calm. And goodbye. I suggest you get in touch with Geoffrey Linton right away – perhaps you had that intention in your mind in any case. I hope you have good news of your sister. And, incidentally, do not leave your house, Mr Maidment. I shall be telephoning you with further instructions later.'

The line went dead, and Maidment let the receiver drop on to its rest. There was no longer any margin for doubt – or hope. Derek had been kidnapped. But why? For God's sake, why? Perhaps he'd learn when the man next phoned. In the meantime . . .

He went to the cabinet where he kept his liquor, and poured himself a strong whisky. He drank it neat. When he felt its warmth hit his belly he poured a second, but didn't drink it. He sprawled in a chair, his feet on a stool, the glass on a table beside him. Clearly he must plan his conversation with his brother-in-law quite differently. There was no longer any question of appealing for Geoffrey's help. He dared not tell the truth; the threat to Derek was too great. So, what was he to do?

Maidment found himself staring fixedly at the painting over the mantel, Sarah as he remembered her, with Derek – a younger, more childlike Derek – standing beside her. It had been a present from Peter Bingham, an old friend and Derek's godfather. Peter was an accomplished amateur painter, and he had caught the likenesses admirably. The painting brought back a host of memories, and Maidment drew in a sharp breath. He had lost Sarah. He would not jeopardize Derek too. He would do anything, anything, rather than that.

But Bingham, he thought suddenly – Bingham! If he needed an ally, surely he had one in Peter. Geoffrey would want to call in the police, to go through channels, but Peter wouldn't necessarily react like that. What was more he was right here in Switzerland; he called himself a First Secretary at the British Embassy in Berne, though Maidment had a shrewd suspicion that his real job was a little more complex than that. Peter's appointments, since he had joined the Foreign Office, seemed to have been connected with intelligence and security, and there was little reason to doubt that such activities still formed a major part of his career.

Yes, if it came to it, Peter was the man. Understanding, with a personal stake because of his affection for Derek – and not hidebound like Geoffrey. For the moment, however, Maidment thought, he would do as he had been told and appeal to no one. Really he had little choice. He could only hope that the demands to be made on him – financial, professional, whatever – would not be too great, and that he could accede to them with a reasonably clear conscience. Not that his conscience mattered a damn compared with Derek's life.

Taking his whisky with him Maidment returned to the telephone. He tried the Lintons' number but there was no reply. Then he called the Home Office. Geoffrey Linton wasn't available. His wife had been involved in a car accident, and he had gone to the hospital. No one seemed to know which hospital.

*

For Rory Maidment the afternoon passed slowly – excruciatingly slowly. He forced himself to eat, though half an hour later he couldn't have said what he'd eaten, and he drank cup after cup of instant coffee. In the intervals of trying to contact Geoffrey at his home and his office, he wandered vaguely round the house.

33

About four o'clock his phone rang just as he had put it down after yet another such vain attempt. He breathed a sigh of relief as he heard Geoffrey's voice, but at first their conversation was mutually incomprehensible.

'Derek's reached you safely? Julia was so worried he –'

'Thank God it's you. How's Julia?'

'I've been worried too, since she told me.'

'Is she badly hurt?'

'Is he all right?'

'Yes. No. I mean –'

'What the hell do you mean, Rory? Has Derek arrived safely or not? Julia must have been out of her mind sending him off with a strange woman. But, wait a minute, why are you asking after Julia? If you know about the accident, Derek must have arrived.'

Maidment took a deep breath. He was thankful that he wasn't face to face with Geoffrey, and he was thankful that Geoffrey had himself leapt to the obvious conclusion. Somehow acquiescence was easier than lying. 'As you say, Derek's arrived safely, thank you, Geoffrey,' he said. 'He was a bit shaken by the accident, but otherwise he's fine. He says Mrs Carpenter was very kind and – and – efficient. But what about Julia?'

'Well, that's a relief – about Derek, I mean. Julia? Julia didn't get off so lightly.' Linton's voice was rough with anger. 'Cuts and bruises and suspected concussion. She's got some broken ribs and she's hurt her leg. They had to operate to get a bit of metal out of it.'

'Oh, God! I'm sorry.'

'If I could get my hands on the bastards that did it . . . I expect Derek's told you the details. The police say they were high on drugs. Their van stank of cannabis. Rory, let me speak to Derek.'

The request was totally unexpected and Maidment, taken unaware, said the first thing that came into his head. 'I'm sorry, but you can't. Not now. He's – he's in bed.'

'In bed? In the middle of the afternoon?'

'Yes.' He was committed now. 'The doctor gave him a mild sedative. I told you, Geoffrey, he's fine, but he's had a bit of a shock. He's only a kid, you know.'

'Yes. Yes, I do, but – All right. I'll phone again tomorrow. The police have the van, probably stolen, but they'll want anything Derek can give them about the driver and the chap with him. Julia doesn't remember much.'

'I – I see.'

'I'm not going to let the matter rest, Rory. I want those bastards found and punished. Julia could have been killed, and Derek too. As it is, she's been badly hurt, and the car's a write-off. They won't get away with it.'

Geoffrey Linton went on for another couple of minutes in the same strain before he said goodbye. Maidment scarcely listened. He was recognizing his instinctive fear of the kidnappers' reaction if the men in the van should be caught. Unwittingly he knew he had joined the kidnappers' side. He could only hope that it was also Derek's side.

Four

For the second time that Friday Arndt Gunther was at Cointrin Airport. He had changed his windbreaker for a suit, parted his hair on the opposite side and discarded his spectacles. It was not a serious attempt at disguise, but the difference in his appearance between now and this morning was sufficient to throw doubt in the mind of anyone who might have seen him on both occasions.

He had come to meet Trina Hansen off an afternoon flight and, like Maidment earlier that day, expected no extra delays from the obviously increased security precautions, for Trina too was travelling direct from London. She appeared among the first of the passengers, looking radiant in a beautifully-cut spring suit; she had no qualms about spending her father's money on herself, as well as on her cause. Gunther regarded her with approval.

They embraced and kissed. They might have been lovers meeting. In fact, they were, in the true sense of the phrase, merely good friends, at least most of the time. Gunther would have wished it otherwise, but he knew he hadn't a hope as long as Horst Zabel was around, and he accepted the situation, though physically he was better-looking than Zabel, taller, stronger, just as well educated. His background was typical of a certain kind of German terrorist: professional family, university and medical school till he had 'dropped out', as they used to say, to join a group. Then, a period of serious indoctrination and training, employment as a courier, a support role in the occasional operation . . .

What he lacked, Gunther admitted, was Zabel's personality, his determination, his *Weltanschauung* – his view of the world – that enabled him to surmount almost any obstacle in pursuit of his objectives. Still, better a crust . . ., he thought, glancing at Trina. Besides, for him, as for all the members of the Zabel group, there were more important things than sex.

'You've changed the car,' Trina Hansen said as she got into a blue BMW.

'This one's great – lots of power, but I can't pretend it was a bargain,' Gunther laughed, 'except it produced a dividend. In other words, I've found us a garage, a small place. Middle-aged chap, on his own, eager for a quick buck with no questions asked. He'll do whatever we want. I suggested tonight, and he was happy.'

'Tonight? Then you feel sure of Maidment?'

Gunther shrugged. 'I told you on the phone his reactions were what we expected. Disbelief, anger, fear – but mostly fear. Anyway, there's no point in delay, is there?'

'Have you given Maidment his orders?'

'Not yet. He's standing by. If you'd prefer . . .' Gunther glanced questioningly at Trina.

The decision was hers. 'No,' she said. 'We'll go ahead. But don't tell him more than you have to. Anyone in his situation could be unpredictable.'

For a while there was silence between them. Gunther drove with casual competence. He had moved from the rooms he had been occupying to an hotel close to the Parc de la Grange. It was a respectable place, not inexpensive – from most rooms you could see the *Jet d'eau* for which Geneva was famous – but large enough to be incurious about two young visitors from Zurich. He had resisted the temptation to book a double room.

'Any news of Horst?' he asked, breaking the silence as they crossed the Pont du Mont-Blanc.

'He's looking forward to Easter.'

Trina smiled to herself. She was glad to be out of England.

She hadn't enjoyed that morning's part of the operation. The Maidment boy had turned out to be a bloody brat! Not that he'd caused any real trouble after she'd hit him. He had gone into the house without protest, and he had made no fuss when he was locked in the room upstairs. Anyway Nana Smith would deal with him; after all, she had once been a professional nanny and she knew how to cope with recalcitrant youngsters. And he'd be safe with Nana as long as he was needed, which would be just as long as he was useful to Horst.

'That gives us about ten days,' Gunther said.

Trina nodded. Ten days, she thought, and then there must be no mistake. They would get no second chance.

*

Derek Maidment was curled up on the window seat of his third-storey room, looking out at the sun setting beyond a distant belt of trees. He knew he was somewhere in the south of England, but that was about all he did know. When he had finally overcome his fear and scrambled up from the floor of Mrs Carpenter's car they had been driving along country lanes – pretty, leafy lanes, but lanes he had never seen before.

However, it was clear that Mrs Carpenter knew where she was going, for suddenly they swung through a gate and the house was in front of them. It was obviously isolated, and its dirty brick walls and untidy front garden were not at all inviting. If it had a name Derek never saw it. He was too busy staring at the woman who opened the front door.

Nana Smith was worth staring at. She was just under six feet tall, and, though in her seventies, was ramrod straight. Her grey hair was drawn back from a severe face and knotted into a bun. She used no make-up and her clothes were plain – a white blouse and a navy blue skirt – but she made one concession to vanity. She wore a double string of pearls around her neck.

'So this is the boy,' she said, her voice surprisingly deep.

'Yes. His name's Derek, and I warn you, Nana, he's not as harmless as he looks.'

'He'll be all right with me.'

For a moment Derek had taken her words literally, and almost believed them. In spite of her forbidding appearance Nana, as she told him to call her, was far more reassuring than Mrs Carpenter. But she'd locked him up in this room, and left him. He'd had nothing to eat since breakfast, and by now he was hungry, none too warm, unutterably lonely and miserable.

Shortly after two by his watch he thought he heard a car drive away. He had hoped that Mrs Carpenter was leaving and that Nana might now bring him something to eat, but no such luck. The house seemed silent and empty and frightening.

He had been sensible enough to explore his surroundings in detail. The door which gave on to the rest of the house was solid and locked, but the room itself was not uncomfortable. It had a carpet on the floor and was furnished as a bed-sitting room, with a divan, an armchair, and a built-in wardrobe; a second door led to a minute windowless room with a shower, a wash-basin and a lavatory. All the cupboards and drawers were empty, and there were no books. He refused to unpack his own bag that Nana had brought up for him; it would have been an admission that he was here to stay.

The main room had one window, firmly locked, and Derek had spent the rest of the afternoon on the window-seat, gazing down at the walled garden below and the rolling countryside beyond. There were no actual bars on the window, but even if he broke the glass there was no way down – no drainpipes, no trees nearby, nothing but a twenty-five foot drop to what seemed to be a stone patio of some kind. Derek thought about the extraordinary events of the day. He wept a little and slept a little. He didn't hear the car return.

Nana Smith had driven Trina to Heathrow to catch her flight to Geneva, then done some shopping and gone to her doctor. She'd had a long wait, but to no avail. The results of her tests hadn't come through yet. She was glad to get home.

She put on the kettle, and went upstairs to collect the boy. He would be needing his tea. She wouldn't forget Trina's warning, but there was no call for needless unkindness. Missing his lunch had been enough punishment for his pointless attack on Trina in the car. You couldn't really blame him, and he must have been surprised when her wig came off. Nana smiled to herself. Anyway, it would mean too much work to keep him locked away all the time; she wasn't paid to carry endless trays up and down those stairs.

★

It was later the same evening, but still light, when Trina dropped Arndt Gunther on the Rue de Haut some fifty yards beyond the house where Rory Maidment lived. Gunther walked back, paused at the entrance to the courtyard to light a cigarette, and went on.

He had seen nothing suspicious, nothing to alert him, but then he wouldn't. If Maidment had called in the police they would wait till he got into the car, so that they could at least hold him for intent to steal. Alternatively, Maidment might himself have arranged some surprise. The risk was unavoidable.

Gunther retraced his steps, shrugging. No use guessing. He could, he supposed, have told Maidment to leave the car parked on the street or on a *Parc de Stationnement*. But traps could be arranged in such places just as easily, and in some ways it added to the pressure on Maidment if he had a chance to see for himself a man genuinely involved with the operation against his son. No, he must rely on the overwhelming threat to ensure that Maidment had done as he was told.

Grinning to himself as he recalled the lectures he had

attended on such subjects as 'Terrorist and Victim: Their Likely Reactions', Gunther walked boldly into the courtyard. Rory Maidment had been told to stay upstairs, and he was doing so, though, as Gunther had surmised, he hadn't been able to resist the temptation to stand well back from the window to watch the proceedings, to get some idea of the kind of criminal responsible for kidnapping Derek. He was a little disappointed to find that Gunther, head well down, was such an undistinguished figure.

Gunther turned the handle and pulled the garage door up and over. It came easily. The big Jaguar was standing there, key in the ignition. Gunther didn't hesitate. A quick glance round and he was behind the wheel. He backed out through the courtyard, and into the Rue de Haut. As he passed Trina, waiting in the BMW, he gave a thumbs-up signal. Maidment had seemingly obeyed his instructions to the letter.

With Trina following, Gunther drove eastwards towards the Gare des Eaux-Vives. In a back street nearby was a garage, its windows filthy, its sign rusting. Either its proprietor had lost all ambition, or he had his own reasons for not wishing to appear opulent. Certainly in such a poor location he couldn't have expected much normal business.

However, behind the small forecourt, with its neglected petrol pumps, was a well-equipped car body workshop, as Gunther had discovered. Its big doors were open, and he drove straight in, followed by Trina. Monsieur Le Gros, breathing garlic, came forward to greet them.

'You said some – er – adjustments to an automobile, monsieur.' He regarded Trina with veiled interest. 'You didn't mention that the car would belong to someone in the *Corps Consulaire*.' He pointed to the 'CC' on the licence plates.

'So what?' Gunther was brusque. 'More expensive, perhaps.'

'I'm sure monsieur understands. But I'll leave it to his generosity.'

'Right. Let's get on with it, then. Here are the specifications of what we want done.' He passed the *garagiste* a piece of paper, which the men frowned over for several minutes. Gunther grew impatient. 'Come on, monsieur. We don't have all night. Can you do the job, or would you prefer us to find someone else?'

Le Gros regarded him sardonically. 'It might not be too easy for monsieur to find someone he could trust with such a task, especially if time is of the essence.'

'Can you do it or not?' Gunther's French became more guttural as he grew more exasperated.

'Yes, monsieur, I can do it. I was just thinking about the upholstery, which is a specialized job, but I can deal with that from inside the boot without disturbing its appearance –'

Trina interrupted him. 'Good. So you'll do it for us, monsieur, and we'll pay you double what we promised. Agreed?'

They shook hands. *'D'accord.* If you will come back at one a.m., say, it will be finished.'

'We'll wait,' Gunther said. 'Maybe I can help you to get it done more quickly.'

Le Gros shrugged. 'As you wish, monsieur. It's really a one-man job because of the confined space, but. . . I'll show mademoiselle the office. If she is to wait too she'll be more comfortable there.'

Five minutes later he had got down to his task and, once started, he didn't waste time. He was competent and neat and careful. Gunther could do little more than pass him tools, and he soon lost interest and joined Trina in the office. Left to himself, Le Gros worked even more efficiently, and just before midnight had finished the task.

'Monsieur! Mademoiselle!' He called to them. *'Voila!* I defy anyone to have done a better job for you – a more inconspicuous job, shall I say?' He stood to one side so that they could admire his handiwork.

The boast, Gunther agreed, was justified. At a superficial

glance, either inside or outside, no one would have guessed that Maidment's car had undergone any modification. Trina added her praise.

'Splendid! A splendid job!' She nodded her satisfaction to Gunther. 'Monsieur Le Gros, I saw you had some cans of beer in your office. Let's go and drink on it. Then we'll settle with you.'

She led the way. There were three cans of beer on the untidy desk beside an old-fashioned cash register. She pushed one towards Le Gros, who opened it and drank thirstily.

'I needed that!' he said, putting down the can and wiping his mouth with the back of his hand. 'But you're not drinking?'

Neither Trina nor Gunther had touched their beer. 'No,' Gunther said. 'Don't you have any glasses?'

'Glasses?' Gunther was surprised. 'Sure. Right here.'

Turning, he bent towards a low shelf, and without hesitation Gunther chopped him across the back of the neck with the side of his hand. There was a sharp click and Le Gros collapsed. Gunther rolled him over with a foot, not bothering to stoop.

'Dead?' Trina asked laconically.

'Of course. And he didn't know a thing. He died happy, the lucky *type*.'

Trina laughed. She was already knocking things to the ground, pushing over a chair, tearing down a poster, creating an impression of vandalism. Gunther stepped over the dead *garagiste* and opened the cash register. He took what little money there was, and left the drawer open.

'That'll do. Let's split,' Trina said.

They switched off the office light and returned to the workshop. They left as they had come, Gunther leading in the Jaguar, Trina following in the BMW.

In the Rue de Haut Maidment's house was in darkness. A cat shot across the cobbles as Gunther drove into the courtyard, but there were no other untoward happenings. Gunther garaged the car, quietly pulled down the garage door and walked away. Trina was waiting for him a few yards along the road. From their point of view it had been a satisfactory evening.

★

But for Rory Maidment it had been an evening of misery and uncertainty. He had scarcely moved from the chair he had drawn up by the window, except to make himself a sandwich and refill his glass. He had been drinking heavily, though he knew he would pay for it with a hangover in the morning. The thought of the next day appalled him.

The voice on the phone had insisted that he should carry on as usual, go to the Savoie to spend the weekend with the Grandins, 'as doubtless he had intended', behave as if Derek's absence was a mere misfortune. He had said he would, but he wasn't sure it would be possible. To spend two days with old Denis who, however infirm his body, had the quick perceptive mind of the educated Frenchman, and pretend to be carefree, would be an enormous strain. To make love to Marie-Louise, and hide his feelings would be . . . He couldn't face it.

Eventually Maidment dozed. He woke with a start and stood, swaying slightly, as Gunther drove into the courtyard. He heard the garage door come down, and watched the shadowy figure leave. He waited a full five minutes by his watch, and when there were no further signs of activity he went downstairs carefully, using the handrail all the way. The liquor he had drunk was getting to him.

He tried to pull himself together as he let himself into the garage by the door which led from the kitchen, and switched on the overhead fluorescent light. Slowly, like a pilot inspecting an aircraft before flight, he walked round his car. It looked exactly as it had always looked. He peered underneath

44

from all angles. Nothing. He opened the deep boot and stuck his head in. The interior was in shadow from the lid, but it seemed to be empty though it had a strange smell – a mixture of sweat and garlic and something else he couldn't place. He wrinkled his nose in disgust.

He opened the door and found the key in the ignition. The position of the driver's seat had been altered, but then he already knew that someone else had driven the car. He had seen the man. How far had he taken it? Pleased with himself for having made a note of the previous kilometrage, Maidment checked the new figure. It seemed that, though the car had been away for several hours, it had been driven only a short distance.

'Mad!' Maidment muttered to himself. 'Mad!' What the hell had they wanted with his car? He opened the glove compartment. It contained, as usual, a plan of Geneva and its environs, a Michelin Guide to Switzerland, a tin of boiled sweets and an old pair of gloves. He peered into the rear of the car, and caught a glimpse of white on the carpet, protruding from the base of the front passenger seat.

Hastily he stretched over, and retrieved it. It was a business card, crumpled and greasy. By the interior light he could see that it read, 'CLAUDE LE GROS. *Garagiste. Réparations des Carrosseries*'. It gave an address, which Maidment promptly looked up on the Geneva street plan. He did a rapid calculation. His head had begun to ache, and he had to do it twice before he was satisfied that the distance to Le Gros's garage near the Gare des Eaux-Vives and back would explain the kilometrage put on his car. It still made no sense, but somehow the discovery seemed to Maidment to be a minute triumph. A small hope grew that perhaps he could outwit these vile people and recover Derek safely.

Five

Rory Maidment woke from his drunken sleep, turned over, groaned and buried his head under the duvet. It was no use. The wretched noise continued to nag. He put out an arm, found the clock on the bedside table and tried to turn off the alarm. He had forgotten to set it, he discovered. But if not the alarm, it must be the phone. And, in God's name, who would call him in the middle of the night?

The telephone! Memory came flooding back. Pushing aside the duvet he sat up. Searing pain shot through his temples, but he ignored it. He grabbed at the receiver.

'Yes! Maidment here. Who is it?'

'At last! The phone's been ringing and ringing. Why didn't you answer?'

'Oh, it's you, Geoffrey.' Maidment leant back against the pillows. He swallowed hard. He had been afraid, but he had been hoping, too . . .

Light was creeping around the edges of the curtains and he realized that it couldn't still be night. Indeed, the digital clock read 0915. It must be morning, but with the time difference it would be only eight-fifteen in England, early for Geoffrey to be phoning, unless. . . 'What is it? Is something wrong?' He realized as he asked the question that it struck an absurd note.

'Wrong? Of course something's wrong.' Geoffrey Linton had slept badly and he was not in the best of tempers. 'Remember? Julia's in hospital. Her car's a wreck. The police are surprisingly interested and – What on earth's the matter with you, Rory? You sound half asleep.'

46

'Sorry. I've just woken up and I've a rotten hangover.'

'Hangover? But –'

Rory Maidment could picture his brother-in-law frowning fiercely and running a hand through his thinning grey hair. Linton didn't suffer fools gladly, and to him a hangover would seem ridiculous in the circumstances. How could Rory have a hangover when he'd presumably spent the previous evening at home with an ailing Derek? Hurriedly Maidment corrected himself.

'I mean I've a sinus headache. It's the pollen at this time of year. In effect it's the same as a hangover. Makes me slow on the uptake.'

'I see,' said Linton, making it clear that he didn't see at all. 'Well, I promised I'd phone you this morning. I called the hospital a short while ago. Julia's had a reasonable night and they say she's in quite good form. I'll be going to visit her later.'

'That's great, Geoffrey. Give her my love, please. Say how sorry I am about the accident. Derek's love, too,' Maidment added as an afterthought.

'Yes, indeed. Derek's had a good sleep and he's all right, I hope. Can I speak to him? As I told you yesterday, Rory, there are one or two questions.'

This time Maidment was prepared for the request. He had made a silly mistake in admitting to a hangover, but now, in spite of the throbbing in his temples and a queasy feeling in his stomach, he was wide awake and alert. He knew he couldn't afford to be careless; Geoffrey Linton wasn't the kind of man to be easily deceived.

'I'm afraid you can't, Geoffrey. That accident yesterday shook him more than I realized, and I'm not having him reminded of it. It's best forgotten as far as the boy's concerned.'

'Maybe, but the police aren't going to accept that.'

'They've got no choice. I'm not having him questioned, Geoffrey, by you or anyone. He had dreadful nightmares about it last night – all about a big van coming out of nowhere and crashing into them. Besides, he can't be any help. He told me he never saw the driver, or the chap with him.'

'That's a pity. We'd hoped –'

'Can't Julia describe them?'

'No. All she's got is a vague impression of a big man in one of those cotton painter's caps, and that's not much use.'

'No.' Relieved that his lies had been accepted, Maidment could think of nothing more to say. He yearned for the conversation to end, but he didn't want to be the first to break it off. 'We – ell,' he said once hesitatingly, but Linton didn't take the hint, and as he talked on, Maidment, who was normally fond of his brother-in-law, for once wished him in hell.

★

It was mid-morning when Rory Maidment threw his bag on the back seat of the Jaguar and set off for Savoie and the Grandins' house on the edge of Lac d'Annecy, where these days he often spent his weekends. He turned the ignition key with some hesitation, but he reminded himself that, even in the unlikely event that some terrorist gang wanted to plant a bomb in his car, they would hardly go to the lengths of kidnapping Derek to give themselves the opportunity.

Maidment usually took the Autoroute towards Chamonix, crossing the border near Annemasse on the outskirts of Geneva, and a few kilometres further on turning south on A41, which led to Annecy and eventually to Grenoble. This route, he thought, was particularly convenient today, as it meant leaving Geneva to the east, past the area of the Gare des Eaux-Vives. But first he loitered for some minutes around the winding streets of the old town, trying to make sure he wasn't being followed.

His immediate objective was Monsieur Le Gros's garage. He planned to have a look at the premises and, if possible, have a word with the proprietor and sum him up. It was just possible that he could be persuaded or bribed to provide some information about what had been happening. At least it was worth trying.

He left his car, which seemed to be running perfectly, a couple of streets away from the garage, and walked. On a Saturday morning he expected a certain amount of activity, even in this rather depressing neighbourhood. The garage, however, had every appearance of being shut. The pumps were locked, and no one came in answer to the bell beside them. He regarded the establishment's peeling paint and general air of dilapidation. Clearly the business was not prosperous.

A workman, his bag of tools over his shoulder, went by, and Maidment called to him, 'Monsieur, do you know when this place opens?'

The man shrugged. 'Who knows, monsieur? That one opens when he thinks he will. There were lights on when I passed after midnight last night, so he's probably sleeping in this morning.'

'Thanks,' Maidment said.

He glanced up at the windows towards which the man had gestured. Evidently Monsieur Le Gros lived over the garage, and he wasn't anxious for business. Maidment found another bell push by the garage doors, and pressed his thumb on that for a full minute. When there was still no response, he abandoned his plan and returned to his car, annoyed to have wasted so much time.

He was more annoyed when he saw the activity at the frontier. The security alert occasioned by the recent attempt to kill the French president was still in progress, and the French and Swiss border guards were less casual than usual. But he had no trouble and was waved through without delay when it came to his turn. By now it was a beautiful day, clear and sunny, though with a reminder of snow in the chill wind off the mountains. As he negotiated the Autoroute intersection beyond Findrol, and put his foot down for the short drive south, he thought how happy he would be if Derek were beside him.

★

The Grandins lived a few kilometres south of Annecy itself, on the west side of the lake near a large village called Sevrier. Their villa was one of astonishing ugliness. The roof sloped in several directions. Additional rooms jutted at surprising angles. The windows were asymmetrical, without rhyme or reason. The front door was tucked away on one side, as if ashamed of its mean appearance. Denis Grandin, who had inherited the house from an uncle, was convinced it had been designed by a myopic architect.

Nevertheless, the garden was pleasant and the view of the lake magnificent. Grandin had been a lawyer in Paris – a *juge d'instruction* – and on his retirement he had at first been unwilling to leave the city. But at that time Marie-Louise, his only child, was working for the United Nations at the Palais des Nations in Geneva, and it had seemed a sensible move for an ageing widower. Now, though he still missed Paris, he had come to like the people and countryside of the Haute-Savoie.

For Marie-Louise, who had given up her job to look after him when he had had a stroke a year ago, it was a different matter. Grandin knew she was lonely, and missed the companionship of people of her own age. Rory Maidment's regular visits meant a lot to her. And to himself, too, Grandin admitted; he liked Maidment. He hoped he would also like Maidment's son – what was his name? Derek, yes – when he met him, and especially he hoped that Marie-Louise would. Her growing attachment to the Englishman was only too evident, and he was naturally anxious that her life with Maidment and Derek – if it ever came to that – should be a happy one.

Grandin went into the kitchen, with its stone-flagged floor

50

and its array of coloured pots and pans. Marie-Louise, a tall girl in her early thirties, dark-haired and green-eyed, was standing by the stove carefully tasting a stew. Her father sniffed appreciatively at the delicate aroma filling the air.

'The smell by itself's enough to make me hungry.'

Marie-Louise laughed. 'Not long now. It's almost time for an aperitif. Rory's late today.'

'Perhaps he's not coming.'

'Why should you say that? He said he'd come – and bring his boy. If something had happened he'd have phoned.'

'He's not usually so late. Perhaps the boy doesn't want to come, and Rory doesn't know what excuse to make.'

'Ah, Papa, you know perfectly well Rory's not like that.' She mocked him, but there was an element of apprehension in her voice. 'Rory'll be here,' she assured herself.

Less than ten minutes later there was the crunch of gravel under tyres, and Marie-Louise flung a triumphant glance at her father. Then, pulling her blue-and-white striped apron over her head, she ran to the door. Grandin followed more slowly. He was in time to see Marie-Louise draw away from Maidment's embrace, and he hurried forward, hand outstretched.

'Welcome, Rory. Welcome, as always.'

'*Bonjour*, Monsieur Grandin. It's good to be here, as always.'

'Rory hasn't brought Derek,' Marie-Louise said.

'Ah, that's a disappointment. Why is it?' Grandin looked inquiringly from Marie-Louise to Maidment.

Marie-Louise shrugged. 'I've no idea.'

'That's because I haven't had a chance to explain.'

Maidment did his best to speak lightly. He knew that Marie-Louise had been anxious about her first meeting with Derek, that she was eager for the boy to like her. He hated to have to tell lies to her, especially on such a subject. To give himself a moment, he turned his back, and collected his bag from the rear seat of the Jaguar.

'Derek's still in England,' he said. 'I don't think he'll make it to Geneva these holidays. He's got mumps.'

'Mumps! Oh, *le pauvre enfant*! Measles at Christmas and mumps at Easter. That's terrible, Rory.'

Maidment found Marie-Louise's quick sympathy harder to take than her former unexpressed suspicion that he didn't really want her to meet his son. 'Yes, it's bad, but most kids get these complaints. Better now than when he's grown up.'

He hadn't meant to sound unfeeling, but it was clear from the lift of Grandin's shaggy eyebrows and from Marie-Louise's refusal to meet his gaze that they considered his comment unsympathetic in the extreme. If only they knew, he thought miserably, fearing that the weekend was going to be even worse than he had expected.

★

At first his fears were justified. Almost inevitably, it seemed, tension grew as the day progressed. After an early supper Grandin was collected by a friend who regularly partnered him in a bridge foursome, and Marie-Louise was left alone with Maidment. She attacked him at once.

'Then you won't be here for Easter, Rory, as we'd hoped.'

'I – er – I don't know.'

'What do you mean, you don't know? Surely you'll be going to England. You can't not visit your poor son when he's ill. That would be –' She searched for a suitable English word. '– be heartless of you.'

'It all depends.'

'On what? Are you afraid of getting mumps yourself, Rory?' Marie-Louise laughed, but it was a forced laugh. 'They say that sometimes mumps are as bad as castration for a male.'

'I don't think it's quite as bad as that, Marie-Louise. Impotence, yes, but castration, no. Anyway, I've had mumps. You don't get them twice.'

Maidment spoke a little curtly. How could he explain that

52

his movements were totally dependent on what a voice might say over the phone. He couldn't even lie, say he was in fact going to England, because the voice could conceivably tell him to come to Savoie. Whoever they were, they knew about the Grandins. It was one of the things that had shocked him, that they seemed to know so much about his private life.

They continued to bicker until Marie-Louise said, 'I'm going to bed, Rory. You know where the whisky is, if you want one. Papa will be home soon.'

'Darling –'

But she ignored the appeal, avoided his outstretched hand and made for the door. 'I'm tired, Rory. I'll see you in the morning. Good-night.'

Maidment didn't try to stop her. Grimly he helped himself to a whisky and drank it. He told himself that in the circumstances he was fortunate to avoid the intimacies of love-making, but he didn't believe it. He meant to go to his room before Grandin returned, but the old man anticipated him.

'*Une boisson*, Rory?'

'I've already had a night-cap, Monsieur Grandin, thank you.' Maidment indicated his glass.

'Then have another. If you'll forgive me for saying so, you don't seem in your best form today.'

'Unfortunately I'm suffering from a hangover. Too much to drink last night.'

'*Tu essaie noyer ton chagrin*, Rory?' Maidment didn't answer, and Grandin went on. 'I know it's none of my business, but we're friends, I hope, and if you've got sorrows to drown, I'd like to help. You *are* in trouble, aren't you?'

Maidment reacted automatically. 'Trouble? What makes you –'

Grandin interrupted. 'Your general – edginess. And the fact that someone was asking questions about you a week or so ago.'

'Who? What sort of questions?'

Maidment knew his instant response was a confirmation of Grandin's suspicions, but he didn't care. He learnt that a man between thirty and forty, of nondescript appearance, posing as a security officer from the British Embassy, had checked that he was indeed a frequent visitor to the Grandins.

'Now,' said Grandin. 'Tell me.'

Still Maidment hesitated. Grandin had been a *juge d'instruction* – an examining magistrate, an officer of the Court under the French system. To what extent would he still feel bound by his oath?

'In confidence, Monsieur Grandin? *True* confidence? A life may depend on it.'

Grandin saw the point at once. He nodded. 'I'm far removed from my old life, Rory. I'll help if I can, but otherwise –'

It was enough. With relief, Maidment told his story. 'And that's all,' he concluded. 'I'm sorry you've been involved, monsieur. I'll not come here again unless – unless I'm ordered to. You understand that I must put Derek's safety before anything else?'

Grandin, who had listened in silence, nodded again. 'You must come here when you want,' he said gravely, 'but I would ask you to tell Marie-Louise what you've told me. It would be a great pity if this should lead to unnecessary misunderstanding between you, much better she should share your troubles with you. Your secrets will be as safe with her as they are with me. Trust her. Please.'

'I do, but . . .'

'Then go to her now. She may have gone to bed, but I doubt if she's asleep. And, Rory, don't forget: we are your friends.'

'I know and I'm grateful, Monsieur Grandin. I'll take your advice. Thank you.'

*

It had been good advice, too, Maidment thought as he drove back to Geneva on Sunday evening. He had knocked on Marie-Louise's door, and she had reluctantly let him in. He had sat on her bed, and poured out his tale. She had reacted immediately by reaching out her arms and pulling him down beside her. Then, as he began to unbutton his shirt, she had stopped him, and become the practical Frenchwoman.

'How well did you inspect your car?' she had asked.

'Well, it was at night, but in the garage where the light's not bad,' he had replied.

'We'll have a good look in daylight,' she had said decidedly. 'Now come to bed.'

From then on she had shown all the love and understanding he should have known she would.

And next morning in the bright sunlight of the Haute-Savoie, Marie-Louise and her father had been both efficient and encouraging. Between them they had opened all the doors and the bonnet and the boot, and gone over the car with a fine-tooth comb. It was Marie-Louise who had noticed that the back of the rear seat seemed less luxuriously comfortable than usual. Then Maidment had realized that the boot was smaller – less deep – than it should have been. It took only a few more minutes to discover the four minute bolts that held a false substitute bulkhead in place just behind the front of the rear wheel arches.

It was a superb piece of workmanship, covered with the same grey cloth as the rest of the boot. Only the most rigorous inspection would reveal it, and this car with its 'CC' plates was unlikely to receive such treatment. Once the new wall was removed, it uncovered – in the absence of most of the back seat padding – a space the width of the car, half a metre or more deep at the bottom, and nearly a metre high.

'Drugs?' Grandin had said at once. 'Or firearms?'

'I don't know,' Maidment had replied. 'But at least I know where to look. Thank you. Thank you again.'

For the rest of the day they had tried to forget the matter.

He was glad he had told them, Maidment decided, as he drove fast towards the border on Sunday evening. Once more it was clear that security, especially entering Switzerland, was very tight, and small queues of cars were waiting. But, as usual, the Swiss border guard recognized the car and its driver and waved him through without even a glance at his passport.

Once safely across the frontier Maidment turned on the radio, tuned to a local Geneva station. For a few minutes there was music, some piano concerto that Maidment heard only as a background to his thoughts. Then there was a newsflash: one Monsieur Le Gros, a *garagiste*, had been attacked in his office some time during the weekend and killed. The police believed that the motive was theft. Anyone who . . .

Rory Maidment was listening no longer. Not thieves, he knew, but the people who held Derek, obviously covering their tracks. This was irrefutable evidence they were prepared to kill. He had no option but to go along with them.

Six

The next morning Rory Maidment went into the office. His arrival was greeted with surprise on all sides. Why was he there? Wasn't he supposed to be on leave? Where was his son? The questions came fast, but none of them was particularly probing. His explanation was readily accepted; after all, it was perfectly reasonable, and he received a great deal of sympathy on Derek's behalf. The reaction of his secretary, Jean Rodway, a young Foreign Service employee on her first posting abroad, was typical.

'Poor little boy,' she said. 'How miserable for him. Mumps are horrid. And miserable for you, too, Mr Maidment – that he can't come, I mean. You'll be going to the UK for Easter, then?'

'Possibly, Jean. I haven't made up my mind yet,' Maidment replied shortly.

He was sifting through his 'in-tray', but he didn't miss the girl's surprised expression. It was sensible of him not to waste a week's leave – a week he might be able to spend with Derek later in the year – but there was no reason on earth why he shouldn't fly over to visit his sick son during the Easter break. Perhaps other fathers might have considered they had a good excuse for a free weekend, but that wasn't Rory Maidment's kind of reputation. Everyone knew that it was out of character for him not to put the boy first, to consider Derek before his own convenience. With this in mind, his secretary had reacted just like Marie-Louise.

'What happened about that woman who insisted someone had stolen her passport from her hotel room?' he asked, to change the subject.

He wasn't really interested. Missing passports were a routine feature of a consulate's work, and normally such cases would be handled by the clerks. However, because her husband was a well-known British industrialist, he had interviewed this woman himself, and been convinced that she was lying. Why, he couldn't imagine. There was no reason on earth why she should want to sell a passport. It was one of those small mysteries that would probably never be solved, and today he couldn't care less. He barely listened to what Jean was telling him.

Because he had planned to be on leave, Maidment had made no appointments, but there was plenty of paper-work to occupy him, and from time to time members of his staff came in. He did his best to concentrate on their queries and to avoid obvious irritation, but as the day dragged on he found the demands of his job more and more of an effort.

During the afternoon Hugh Cantley, the Consul-General and his immediate superior, asked to see him to discuss problems posed by recent staff reductions, and he was in his chief's office when Jean Rodway knocked. Clearly embarrassed, she stood just inside the door, and apologized profusely for interrupting them.

'I'm terribly sorry, sir, but there's a lady on the phone who says she must speak to Mr Maidment. A Mrs Carpenter. I asked her to leave a number, but she refused. She said to fetch Mr Maidment, wherever he was. She said he'd be very angry if I didn't get him.'

'A determined female, evidently, this Mrs Carpenter.' The Consul-General's smile was wry. Hugh Cantley was newly-arrived in post; he was a big, quiet man, rather shy, but seemingly shrewd. 'Do you know her, Rory?'

For a moment Maidment couldn't speak. That the woman was confident enough to phone him at the Consulate was bad enough, but such an importunate demand was appalling. It demonstrated, he realized, how sure of their position this vile

58

mob was. Suddenly he felt nauseated.

'Rory, are you all right?'

Cantley spoke sharply, and Maidment, unaware of how pale he had become, was startled by the question. 'Yes – er – yes. I'm fine. Sorry. This Mrs Carpenter – I think it must be about my son.'

'Take it here. Or would you prefer to go back to your office, Rory? We've finished our business for the present, anyway.' The Consul-General was concerned at Maidment's obvious distress. He didn't know Maidment very well as yet, but he knew his subordinate's history and, like everyone else in the office, he had heard about Derek's illness. 'Mumps can be a nasty thing. I hope he's not worse,' he added.

Maidment wasn't aware of making any reply, of leaving the room, of hurrying along the corridor, of entering his own office. It seemed as if he merely found himself standing by his desk, the telephone receiver gripped in his hand, shaking with the effort of controlling his emotions.

'This – this is Rory Maidment, Mrs Carpenter.'

'Ah, at last. I thought they'd find you eventually.'

It was a cool English voice, younger than he had expected, and the hint of amusement behind it infuriated him. His grip on the receiver tightened, but he said nothing.

'You're still there, I hope, Mr Maidment?'

This time she took no trouble to hide her amusement. She was laughing at him, deliberately provoking him.

'I'm here,' he said sharply. He heard a small noise behind him, and turned to find that his secretary had followed him into the room. 'All right, all right,' he said angrily, waving her away. She disappeared quickly. 'He terrified me,' she was to confide later to a friend in the ladies' room. 'He was absolutely furious. I've never seen him like that before.'

Alone, Maidment let his anger erupt. 'In God's name why did you phone me here? Don't you realize this line goes through a switchboard? You're not even using my direct-dial number! How – how is Derek?

59

Trina Hansen laughed aloud. 'Calm down, Mr Maidment. It's just a simple message. Derek's perfectly comfortable. But you must be at home this evening. You'll be phoned at seven, and you'll be able to speak to him. Okay?'

'You mean that?'

'Of course. Goodbye for now, Mr Maidment.'

He heard the click as the line went dead, and he dropped his own instrument back on its stand. He sat at his desk and buried his face in his hands. The woman had said they'd let him speak to Derek. But why should he believe her? He knew they were murderers, casual killers. The thought of his son being dependent on their goodwill was an agony. Nevertheless, in spite of himself his spirits rose at the possibility of hearing Derek's voice, of being able to offer him love and encouragement. If only he could bring himself to offer hope, too.

It was some time before Maidment lifted his head.

★

'Seven days from now and it'll be over,' Trina Hansen said as she left the phone and rejoined Arndt Gunther. 'Easter Monday. Then we shan't need Maidment any more, or his brat.'

'We'll let the boy go?' Gunther asked.

'Yes, Arndt. Why not? If he's returned to his loving father it'll take some of the heat off. Maidment might just accept his good fortune and keep his mouth shut. And anyway we don't want Nana Smith to be the object of a murder hunt when it's not essential.'

They spoke with total indifference, as if they were discussing whether or not to put down a dog which had become a nuisance, but belonged to an aged relative from whom they had expectations. Whether young Derek Maidment lived or died was merely a question of convenience.

Gunther didn't dispute Trina's decision. He said, 'It's

60

going to be a long week.'

'For Maidment, yes.'

For all of us, Gunther thought, and for you in particular. But he didn't say anything. He glanced sideways at his companion, a glance of reluctant admiration. Trina showed no signs of stress.

She had been phoning from a café off the Quai Général-Guisan, nearly opposite the *Jardin Anglais*, and as they began to stroll past the great flower clock, she said suddenly, 'I want to meet this Maidment.'

'Meet him? In person? Why? Is it necessary?'

'Yes. We know a great deal about him, but it's hard to judge him completely without seeing him, speaking to him.'

'*I*'ve seen him. I've been following the bloody man around for days, ever since my car happened to be behind his coming into Switzerland that Sunday.'

'I know, Arndt, I know. And it was absolutely brilliant of you to realize that he might be exactly what we wanted.' Trina put her arm through Gunther's and leaned her body into his as they walked. 'In fact, if we believed in God, we could say Maidment seems to have been a Godsend – a Godsend we'd have missed but for you.'

'It was a stroke of luck, all right.' Gunther grinned. He liked to feel Trina against him, though he knew it meant nothing to her.

'You really want to meet Maidment?'

'Yes. I feel it's important to judge how cool he's likely to be if there's some kind of crisis. I think we can be sure he won't betray us deliberately while the boy's in our possession – he's no fool, and he's done exactly as he's been told so far. But he could panic and . . .'

'Give the game away?'

'It's not a game!' Without warning Trina turned on Gunther fiercely, pulling her arm away from his. Coloured stains appeared under her high cheek bones. 'You . . .' she released a stream of abuse in gutter German.

'For Christ's sake, Trina!' Gunther said, alarmed by this unexpected attack. 'It was only a – a manner of speaking.'

'It's not a manner I like!'

They were standing still, confronting each other in the middle of the pavement outside Patek Philippe's main store. People were moving around in order to pass them, and one or two glanced at them curiously. Gunther was the first to realize they were drawing attention to themselves.

'Come along, Trina,' he said. 'Calm down. You know I didn't mean anything.'

Gunther took her by the elbow and urged her to continue their walk. He was upset, not so much because she had sworn at him, but because of the way her temper had snapped. As they turned off the Quai into the Place Longuemalle he reflected on how he had misjudged her. She wasn't nearly as free from nerves as she appeared. Therefore she was more likely to make mistakes when the time came.

He was almost thinking aloud when he broke the silence that had lasted till they reached the Rue de la Fontaine, and the tower of St Peter's Cathedral had come into view. 'Trina, are you determined to meet this Maidment personally? Couldn't I meet him, if it's really essential? No one ever remembers what I look like – nondescript, that's me. But you – he'd never forget you. I don't like it. It's an additional risk, and we can't afford risks.'

'He won't get a chance to remember me. It won't matter if he meets me again – not with what I've got in mind. But I must see him and talk to him.'

'Okay.' Gunther was not prepared to argue further.

'I'll give him his final instructions myself. Next Friday.' Trina smiled to herself. 'Good Friday.'

'Okay,' Gunther said again.

By now Trina had recovered her composure. She took Gunther's hand, swinging it backwards and forwards as they strolled amongst the tourists past the antique shops and art galleries of the picturesque Place du Bourg-du-Four, with the flower-decked fountain at its centre.

'I know the whole thing's an awful risk, Arndt,' she said. 'We've accepted that from the beginning. But at least we'll have more idea what the real odds are if we've been able to guess at Maidment's reactions in a crisis.'

'Will that help – guessing at the odds?'

'It might. After all, Arndt, you'll be right there behind him, won't you? And if it came to it, I know we can rely on you.' She squeezed his hand.

'Of course,' he said. But he knew that if it did 'come to it' – if he did have to intervene, his chances were slim.

★

Maidment's call came at exactly seven o'clock. He forced himself to let the phone ring three times before he lifted the receiver. At once he recognized the voice as that of the man who had spoken to him before.

'Mr Maidment?' Gunther was calling from Trina's hotel room. 'First, you're doing very well. Keep it up. Behave perfectly normally. Now, your immediate instructions. On Good Friday you make no commitments. Saturday you go to the Grandins, returning to Geneva on Monday evening. Have you got that?'

'Yes, but –'

'No "buts", Mr Maidment. We will be in touch with you on Thursday with more details. Do just as we say, and everyone will benefit. And thank you for the use of your car. I trust you found nothing wrong with it on its return.'

Maidment hesitated. Was he meant to have noticed Monsieur Le Gros's work, or not? 'I've no complaint,' he said, hoping this would be interpreted as the right answer.

Gunther laughed. 'Fine. Just don't get too curious, Mr Maidment. You won't, will you?' He covered the mouthpiece with his hand and said to Trina, who was sitting at the dressing table busy lacquering her nails, 'He's found the compartment.'

'As we expected. He's not a fool.' Trina inspected her handiwork carefully. 'Get on with it, Arndt.'

'About your son, Mr Maidment.'

'Yes. When –'

'Not very long. Be patient, Mr Maidment.'

'How long? Your – your colleague, Mrs Carpenter – she said I could speak to him this evening.'

'So you can. Your phone will ring again soon after I hang up. But remember, the call will be monitored, Mr Maidment. If you ask the boy any leading questions, or if he volunteers anything that could be damaging to us, you'll be cut off immediately. Do I make myself clear?'

'Yes, yes. I understand.'

'Fine. You'll be hearing from us. Goodbye, Mr Maidment.'

If it weren't for the latent threat, it could almost have been a business discussion, Maidment thought, with himself as the junior employee. But that was beside the point. They could treat him any way they liked, if only Derek could be safe. He sat, biting the tip of his thumb, until the phone rang again.

'Rory Maidment here.'

'Good-evening, Mr Maidment.'

Maidment sighed. Not Derek. A woman's voice, but unusually deep. Not Mrs Carpenter. Someone older. 'Good-evening,' he said coldly. 'Who's that?' He didn't expect an answer, but one came.

'I'm Nana Smith, Mr Maidment. Your son, Derek, is staying with me now. He's in good health and I can assure you he's being well looked after, though naturally he'd rather be with his father.'

Maidment had no alternative but to respond. 'I see. Thank you, Mrs Smith.'

'*Miss* Smith. Nana Smith,' she corrected him. 'Here's Derek, Mr Maidment.'

And moments later a small, piping voice said doubtfully, 'Hello, Dad. It's me. Derek.'

'I know. Hello, old man. It's great to hear you. How are you?' Maidment knew his voice was false and over-hearty. He bit his bottom lip hard. He told himself to sound strong and reassuring.

'I'm okay, Dad, but – but I don't understand. If you know I'm here, why can't you come and get me? It's my birthday next week and you promised we'd go ski-ing.'

'I've not forgotten, Derek. But I'm afraid we'll have to postpone the celebration for a while. I realize it's disappointing, and I'm sorry. It's disappointing for me, too.'

'But why? That Mrs Carpenter who brought me here, she was horrid. I pulled off her hair and she hit me. Dad, I don't want to stay here. I want to be with you.'

'Of course you do. And I want you to be with me, Derek, but at the moment it can't be done. We'll get together again as soon as possible. I promise.'

'So I've got to stay here?'

'Yes, for a little while. Is it – very bad?'

'Not really. Nana's kind.' There was a sound on the line that could have been a sob.

Maidment winced. 'Tell me, Derek, what do you do with yourself all day?'

'I help Nana in the house, and she lets me go into the garden. In the evenings we play Scrabble and card games and we watch the telly.'

'That's not too bad then.'

'No.' A pause, and Derek said, 'Is Aunt Julia all right?'

'She's fine,' Maidment lied. 'She's got a few bruises, but no bones broken. You were both lucky in that accident. She and Uncle Geoffrey send their love.'

'Do *they* know I'm here?'

'Yes, Derek. But listen. I can't explain now. You'll just have to accept the situation, but I promise it won't be for terribly long, and then I'll make it up to you. I swear I will.'

Maidment heard himself becoming too vehement, and the polite response of, 'Yes, Dad,' confirmed his fears. Derek no longer trusted him. Maidment was glad when Nana Smith intervened. The goodbyes between father and son were stilted.

'The bastards!' Maidment said aloud. 'The bastards!' But there were no real words for what he felt. At that moment he would have sold his soul to the devil to ensure Derek's safety.

Seven

'Rory's behaving damned oddly, if you ask me. I don't understand it. It's not like him.'

Geoffrey Linton sounded as he felt, exasperated. It was Tuesday evening and he was visiting his wife who, supported by a construction of pillows, was moderately comfortable in her high hospital bed. Her condition was improving rapidly. Her husband had drawn up a chair beside her, and was holding her hand.

'He doesn't seem to care a damn. Whereas other people . . .'

Linton glanced around. Julia smiled. She was surprised by the attention she had received. The aseptic room had been transformed. An over-abundance of flowers, get-well cards, and at least two baskets of fruit had been delivered. Someone had even sent a bottle of champagne, and there had been innumerable telephone calls since word had got around that she was well enough to receive them.

'Everyone's been very kind,' she said.

'Except your dear brother. He was so off-hand when I spoke to him on Saturday, I've not phoned again. All he could think of was Derek. Derek was suffering from shock. Derek was having nightmares. In no circumstances was Derek to be questioned. Derek. Nothing but Derek. No one else mattered. Rory barely remembered to ask after you. Dear God, anyone would think the boy had been badly hurt, and you were to blame.'

'Nonsense, Geoffrey. You're imagining things.'

'Have you heard from him? Has he phoned you? Sent you

flowers?'

'No, but –' Julia admitted to herself that her brother had seemed unusually indifferent to her welfare, but she didn't want Geoffrey to make an issue of it. 'I'm not exactly lacking for attention, am I? Look at all the gifts I've received.'

'Well, you know you've made the news, darling.' He gestured at the newspapers on the table by the window, and the television set facing the bed. In reality, Maidment's behaviour was only a minor worry to him, but it served to cloak his more important concerns. 'The police are very keen to find the jokers who ran into you, and they've given the incident a fair amount of publicity.'

'Yes. It's surprising.' Julia thought of the plain-clothes officer who had spent an hour of his time with her that morning. Some of his questions, such as whether Mrs Carpenter had spoken with a foreign accent, had seemed decidedly curious. She decided not to bother Geoffrey with the point, but, 'Mrs Carpenter has never come forward, has she?' she asked.

'Not as far as I know.' Linton helped himself to one of his wife's grapes and carefully took the pips from his mouth before he added. 'It's a pity. She was closest to the incident. She might be able to identify the men, and she might confirm what the major says, that the accident looked to him to be deliberate.'

'The driver was stoned,' Julia reminded him. 'No one in his senses would have run into me deliberately.'

'I suppose not.'

'The milkman saw the whole thing, too, and he didn't think it was deliberate, did he?'

'No, but apparently he's not the most observant of men. The major, as you might expect, seems to be an excellent witness.' Deliberately Linton chose another grape. 'And so is our Mrs Walker. She didn't see the accident or realize it had happened at the time. But once she learnt of it she was able to give an excellent description of two men – presumably the driver and his mate – pounding down the laneway by our house.'

'I didn't know that.' Julia shifted restlessly, and winced as the wound in her thigh hurt. She didn't really mind whether the men who had caused the accident were caught or not. Derek was all right, even if Rory was over-reacting, and the doctor had said she should be home for Easter. She'd be glad to forget the whole thing.

'Mrs W was upstairs cleaning out Derek's room, and she saw them from his window,' Linton explained. 'Not a good view, but she picked out the big, burly chap from the mug shots the police showed her because of his almost white hair. He's probably an albino.'

'So they know who the thugs are?'

'They seem to have a pretty good idea, yes.' Linton decided he wouldn't tell his wife that the security people had reason to suspect the 'thugs', as she called them, of contacts with an international terrorist gang. There was no point in worrying her unnecessarily, and he had already agreed with the doctor and the hospital staff not to mention that his wife's room was at the end of a corridor and that a plain-clothes man was sitting unobtrusively in an alcove by the window near her door. 'What they've got to do now is find them.'

*

In fact, as a result of a certain amount of leg-work by the CID and the Special Branch, some devious inquiries by the Security Service, and a stroke of luck, the authorities already believed they knew the place where Frank Roth and Bruno Dieke might be found. But they were not certain, and it was unfortunate that the two cars they sent to make a reconnaissance were normally used by the Special Branch for observation and shadowing, and were not true patrol cars, properly equipped for arrests. As it turned out, it was also unfortunate that Roth had gone out to buy food, and Dieke was alone when the unmarked vehicles drove into the mews.

Dieke, watching a soft-porn video, was unaware of their arrival, but the steady buzz of the doorbell below finally penetrated his consciousness. Cursing Roth who, he assumed, had forgotten his key, he ran down the rickety stairs and flung open the door.

The words of abuse he had half-formulated died on his lips when he saw the men standing outside, and the two cars behind them. Instinctively he made to slam the door. The gesture was a mistake. It convinced the police that they had found their men and they acted quickly. Big and strong as he was, seconds later Dieke found himself stretched face-forward against the wall of the garage, his arms spread above him, his legs kicked apart, in the classic position for a rapid body search.

'What the hell's going on?' he demanded. 'Who are you?'

There was a pause. Then the man who appeared to be in charge said, 'Police. We're taking you in.'

'How do I know you're police? And what for? What's the charge?'

'Show him a warrant card, one of you,' the officer said wearily. To Dieke, he added, 'No charge. Not yet. Suspicion of possessing cannabis, if you must have something. I dare say we'll think of others later.'

One of the men had gone upstairs. Dieke could hear his footsteps stumping about. He'd find the joints, sure enough. But that was all he would find, though there was nothing to stop him from planting heroin or coke or anything that took his fancy. Dieke didn't trust the fuzz and these, he felt certain, were no ordinary cops. For one thing, they were armed; he'd felt the hard outline of a pistol as he'd been hustled against the garage wall.

The man came running down the stairs. 'No one there at present, sir, but signs that two, possibly three, have been pigging it together.'

'Damn! Okay. You two wait and see who returns. Give the

70

place a good going-over in the meantime. And you –' Dieke was allowed to stand upright and face them; handcuffs were snapped around his wrists. 'You come along with us.'

'Why? I've done nothing.'

'When do you expect your chum back?'

'What chum?'

'Dark chap. Sallow complexion. Looks as if he's dying of TB. Answers to the name of Frank.'

'Never heard of him,' Dieke said automatically, but, Christ! he thought, they knew Frank's name, probably his too, though they hadn't used it yet. What else did they know? About Trina? The boy? The whole bloody operation . . .

As they rushed him across the cobbles and into the leading car the thoughts in his head were tumbling like laundry in a dryer. Uppermost, however, was the urge to warn Frank at whatever cost, but this meant an attempt to escape – and he had no idea of Frank's exact whereabouts. At the chip shop? Buying beer at the pub?

Dieke stared through the car window as they turned out of the mews. He was sitting in the back on the offside beside one of the men, while the officer whom everyone called 'sir' was in front next to the driver. Suddenly he realized that his cuffs had not been changed to join him to the man beside him; his wrists were still manacled, certainly, but they lay freely in his lap before him. What was more the car door beside him was unlocked, and the interior handle was in place. The pigs had been bloody careless.

Then across the road he saw Frank, coming out of the corner Paki shop that was always open. Obviously he had completed his chores, for he was laden with two bags. Pale-faced, dark hair ruffled by the slight breeze, he started to walk along the opposite pavement in the direction of the mews. He moved neither too fast, nor too slowly, his lips pursed as if he were whistling. And he was going to walk straight into the arms of the pigs' reception committee; he wouldn't have a chance.

Dieke seized his opportunity. The car had stopped in a small jam of traffic at the lights and, almost level with it, Frank Roth was skirting a pram, avoiding a toddler. Dieke lifted his arms and crashed his handcuffs down on the head of the man beside him. Then he burst open the door, and threw himself out of the car into the street, just as the lights changed and the traffic shifted.

'Frank!' he shouted, or believed he shouted. He never saw the bus, whose driver had pushed his foot down on the accelerator the second the green signal showed. He was barely aware of the wheel that seemed to hover momentarily above him before descending.

Roth didn't hear Dieke call to him, but out of the corner of his eye he saw the sudden movement as the white-haired figure rolled from a car, his cuffed wrists held up in front of him. He saw the wheel of the bus pass over the body, and he knew that Dieke had died instantly.

The warning was clear, and Roth didn't miss a stride. While the traffic halted, the woman with the pram screamed, and other pedestrians either ran into the road or stood and gawped, he continued at the same pace with only a casual glance towards the accident.

As he moved on, his view was blocked by the bulk of the bus, which also prevented the police, whose attention was naturally focused on the dead man, from noticing him. He walked past the end of the mews, taking care not to look in, and eventually found a phone box that had not been vandalized.

The conversation was brief. There were no preliminaries. As soon as contact was made, Frank Roth spoke. He was businesslike and unaffected by emotion. The voice at the other end of the line – someone whom Roth had never met – was equally succinct.

'You're sure he's dead?'

'Yes.'

'So they'll be waiting for you?'

'Yes.'

'Then go home. It's possible? You need help?'

'No help.'

'Right. Goodbye and good luck.'

Some hours later Frank Roth reached Harwich, where he boarded the ferry to the Hook of Holland. He had collected a suitcase from the left luggage office at Victoria Station, and changed in a public lavatory. He had a British passport describing him as a journalist, and a reasonable amount of money. His destination, his 'home' where he would rejoin his cell, was Munich.

★

'It seems to be a complete dead end as far as the police are concerned,' Linton said to Julia when he visited her the following evening. 'They're kicking themselves, and justifiably. One villain's dead, thanks to their carelessness, and the other's disappeared. They'll never catch up with him now. Why they wanted to act like that, without setting up a proper operation, I'll never know. They found nothing of interest in the flat, except that a woman had been staying there recently. There were signs of make-up by the wash-hand basin.' Linton felt that he had been speaking as if he were still in the office, and stopped abruptly.

'A woman? A girlfriend, I expect.' Julia shrugged.

'Could be, though I gather females weren't exactly their thing.'

'Is that important?'

'I don't think so. It's just a bit of data from the files, I gather.'

'And how's the policeman who got hurt?'

'He's got a headache!' Linton laughed unsympathetically. 'And he deserves it. So does the Superintendent who was in charge.'

Geoffrey was glancing around the room. 'Those roses,' he

said suddenly. 'They're lovely. Who sent them?' He pointed to a dozen long-stem red roses that stood tall in a glass vase.

'They *are* magnificent. And, guess what – they're from Rory.'

'Are they indeed? So he's surfaced at last.'

'He phoned, too. We had a long chat.'

'Did he say why he'd been so long about getting in touch?'

'Problems at the office, he said. He had to go in. They're short of staff, evidently. It's a shame when he was hoping to give Derek a really wonderful holiday, isn't it?'

Linton's expression made it clear that he considered Maidment's excuse pretty specious, and something in his wife's tone made him glance at her curiously, but he kept his voice carefully neutral. 'Yes, a great shame,' he said. Then he asked, 'You spoke to Derek?'

'No. I – I couldn't.'

'Why on earth not? I'd have thought the boy would have been only too anxious to speak to you.'

'Rory said he wasn't in Geneva, Geoffrey. Apparently, he's at Lake Annecy, staying with Rory's friends, the Grandins.'

Linton shook his head slowly. 'I see. That's a bit odd, isn't it?'

'Not if Rory's really busy, I suppose. Derek'll be better off in the country, and Rory will be joining them for Easter, he says.'

Julia smiled over-brightly. In fact, she was concerned. In conversation, her brother had sounded – 'strained' was the only word to describe her impression – and when she had mentioned it he had offered no explanation, but merely blamed it on the line.

She hesitated before deciding to change the subject. 'What have you done about that dinner party at Number 10 tomorrow week, darling?'

'I cried off. It's disappointing, I know, but clearly you can't go, and the PM understands. We'll be asked again when you're better.' Linton patted his wife's hand. 'Incidentally, we've another invitation for the following Saturday. The Grants want us to go to dinner. I accepted provisionally; it's an informal affair and I thought you might enjoy it.'

'Yes, I'm sure I shall.' Julia hesitated again, wondering once more whether to voice her fears. Then she said firmly, 'Geoffrey, I'm beginning to think you may be right. I'm getting worried about Derek. I agree it's peculiar that neither of us has been able to speak to him. Do you think he's really sick? Could he possibly have been so upset by that accident? Rory did say he was having nightmares, but for my sake he mightn't like to admit the poor child was ill.'

Linton looked at his wife with interest. The same idea had occurred to him, but he had dismissed it. 'No, I doubt it,' he said. 'It's just Rory being over-possessive. You mustn't worry, darling. I'm sure there's nothing wrong with Derek. He's a tough little boy.' He glanced at his watch. 'I must go, darling,' he said. 'Take care.'

'Take care yourself,' she replied as he kissed her.

*

Nana Smith would have agreed with Maidment's assessment of Derek. As far as she could tell, the boy was both tough – and brave. If he cried himself to sleep each night, no one knew; Nana Smith slept on the floor below, and once she had taken her pain-killer and her sleeping pills, she was able to forget him. Safely locked in the attic room, Derek could have screamed till he was hoarse and she wouldn't have heard.

By day, he was quiet and withdrawn. He did as he was bidden. He caused no trouble. For a while after he had arrived on the Friday he had looked for a way of escape, but the front rooms of the house and its front door were all firmly locked, the telephone was kept out of reach, and Nana watched him. In the back, where he was allowed to be outside, he could only go into the garden from which, surrounded as it was by a high stone wall, there was no means of escape. By the Monday he had given up the idea of getting away. He accepted that it was beyond him and pinned all his hopes on being rescued.

He had thought about his father and his Uncle Geoffrey. They would have told the police and everyone would be looking for him. They'd have a description of Mrs Carpenter, though they couldn't know she'd been wearing a wig, and of her car. Surely they'd be able to trace her, and then he'd be found. He had ceased to wonder why anyone should want to kidnap him.

These were his early thoughts. It had been a bitter blow to learn that his family already knew where he was and, for some unknown reason, didn't intend to come for him. He was to stay with Nana Smith indefinitely. Time stretched ahead of him, days of unhappiness to be filled, his birthday forgotten, his return to school ignored – and seemingly no one cared.

He was helping Nana dry the dishes after supper on Wednesday when, lost in his misery, he let a plate fall from his fingers to shatter on the floor. Simultaneously Nana Smith felt an acute pain in her bowels – worse than she had ever suffered. She turned and, in a reflex action, knocked Derek to the ground with a savage blow, cursing him as if he were the cause of her agony.

He lay amidst the bits of broken china. He had cut his hand, but he didn't cry. He stared up at the big, gaunt woman who towered above him. He hadn't understood a word she'd said, because she had sworn at him in German.

Then suddenly she was on her knees beside him, gathering him into her arms. '*Liebchen, liebchen,*' she was saying, 'I'm sorry I hit you.' She tried to explain about the pain that had momentarily blanked out all other considerations. And Derek understood that she hadn't meant to hurt him. He let her cling to him, and even kiss him on the cheek.

'You're a good, good boy, Derek,' she said. 'I won't forget it.'

Eight

Obeying the instructions he had received by telephone the previous evening, Rory Maidment was preparing for a day's outing by strapping his skis to the roof-rack of his Jaguar. He had been eagerly awaiting his orders, but when they came he found them unexpected and surprising.

The days had dragged during the agonizing blank since his unsatisfactory talk with Derek. Only frequent phone calls from Marie-Louise and her father had enabled him to keep up the façade of normality he had been told to maintain. Indeed, it had been Marie-Louise who had reminded him to send flowers to his sister, and persuaded him to call her. His office had been a special problem. He had been going in regularly, but he was certain that his secretary and his colleagues had noticed his preoccupation and the obvious signs of his stress; he could only suppose they had put it down to worry about his son. At least his secretary had had the sense to hint no more about a visit to the UK over the weekend.

The renewal of contact with the kidnappers had come as a relief. Action of any kind was preferable to the suspense of waiting, of the never-ending see-saw between hope and despair. Once he had received his orders he had done his best to consider the situation dispassionately; it was the peculiarity of the orders that had made him finally decide to appeal to Peter Bingham.

He had used the phone in the restaurant where he had dined the night before to call Berne, but even over this presumably secure line had merely told Bingham that he was in a jam and needed help. To his relief, Bingham asked no questions but at once agreed to cancel his own plans for the weekend and do whatever Maidment asked.

'You want me to get there first, and see if anyone's taking an interest in you? You must admit it sounds crazy – but anything you say, Rory. After all, Villars is easy to get to from here, and I always enjoy the ski-ing – and the *après-ski.*'

'For Christ's sake, Peter, it's no joke! It's bloody serious. It couldn't be more serious.'

'Okay, okay.' Bingham was startled; Rory rarely swore. 'Take it easy. You know you can rely on me.'

'Sure. I'm sorry, Peter. I'll explain everything as soon as I get the chance. Meanwhile, be careful at Villars. Be very careful. This thing could turn out to be dangerous as well.'

There was an appreciable pause before Bingham spoke again. 'All right. As I said, it sounds crazy, but nasty situations often are crazy. I'll see you tomorrow, Rory. We'd better have a rendezvous point for later, just in case something goes wrong.'

'Yes. What about the bottom of the main *piste* from Bretaye?'

'Fine.'

'Thanks, Peter. Thanks a lot.'

*

At the time Maidment had felt encouraged by the promise of Bingham's support, but as he drove out of Geneva the next morning, he wondered if he had made a mistake. What could he hope to achieve, even with Peter's help? Maybe he was a fool to play along with the scum who held Derek. Maybe he should have told Geoffrey Linton the truth in the beginning, and involved the authorities, both here and at home. And there was no doubt about the danger. He couldn't forget the cold-blooded killing of Monsieur Le Gros, the *garagiste.* He'd tried to warn Peter, but . . . He must emphasize the warning when they met.

The instructions had been peculiar, but precise. First, on Good Friday, he was to drive his Jaguar to Villars, a popular ski resort at an altitude of about 1,200 metres the other end of Lac Léman, between the Vaudois Alps and the Vallais. The shortest route from Geneva was along the southern, French side of the lake, through Evian-les-Bains, but he had been forbidden to cross any frontiers. This meant a slightly longer journey along the north of the lake, past Lausanne and Montreux. The distance was still quite small – not more than about 120 kilometres – and this route had the advantage of an Autoroute almost all the way.

It was not the finest of days. As Maidment rounded the end of the lake, and entered the valley of the Rhône, there was a hint of mist rolling up, and he wondered if the weather would interfere with what he had been told to do. At least he could be thankful that he was a competent skier.

He left the Autoroute and turned eastwards through Aigle and its surrounding vineyards. A little to the south at Ollon he commenced the steep climb along eight kilometres of hairpin-bends to Villars. Here he parked his car and, skis over his shoulder, made his way to the rack-railway. It was almost the end of the winter season – the artificial skating rink would be closed after the Easter weekend – but Villars was still full of visitors all seemingly enjoying themselves. Only Maidment was alone; as yet he had caught no glimpse of Bingham.

He passed a couple with a small boy who had just come down from the nearby nursery slopes. The boy wore a blue anorak, red pants and a red woollen cap with a long tassel that swung from side to side as he turned his eager face from one parent to the other.

'I did well, Mum, Dad, didn't I?' he demanded.

'Splendidly,' they agreed.

They smiled at each other over their son's head and, because Maidment had obviously overheard, they included

79

him in their proud amusement. Maidment had to force himself to return their smiles. The boy was so like Derek that it hurt.

Perhaps because of the lack of the usual bright sunshine, the restaurant at Bretaye on the peak was half-empty. Maidment had no trouble finding a space for his skis on the rack, and a table by a window for himself. He ordered a half bottle of Veuve Cliquot and some sandwiches, and took stock of his surroundings. At this altitude the haze was not apparent, and the view was magnificent – a panorama of the Dents du Midi and the Muverans range, with Mont Blanc and the peaks of Les Diablerets in the distance. But it was the more immediate prospect that interested Maidment. In the first place, there was still no sign of Peter Bingham, which was a surprise. In the second, it was not easy to visualize Mrs Carpenter and her accomplice among the laughing, chatting people around him. There was just one couple, perhaps, who seemed to be making a determined effort to look as if they had no eyes for anyone other than themselves, but . . .

His instructions had stressed the importance of timing, and he was early. He lingered over his wine, and asked for coffee, drinking two cups slowly. Then he judged the moment had come. He paid his bill and went to collect his skis.

As he carried them out to the smooth trodden snow, the driver of the little ski-train blew his air-horns to announce his departure, and the couple whom Maidment had vaguely suspected hurried from the restaurant. Not them, he thought without surprise, as they climbed into one of the red carriages for the return journey to Villars. Not them, but another couple, a man and a woman he was shortly to meet – a man and a woman whom he hated as he had never hated anyone before.

Maidment shivered. Suddenly it seemed to have got much colder; the soft, white mist was beginning to rise from the valley. He snapped his boots into the bindings on his skis, as below him the little train started to slide away down the mountain, thrust his ski-poles into the snow, and began his own descent.

★

Maidment had been wasting his time trying to spot his enemies at Bretaye. Trina Hansen had out-smarted him. She and Gunther had come up on the cable-car to Les Chaux. They had skied to the edge of the trees and, carefully marking the spot, hidden their skis under a layer of powdery snow, before setting off to trudge through the forest.

Now they waited, within sight of the main ski-run from Bretaye to Villars. They wore dark green anoraks, black ski pants, black woollen caps pulled well down over their ears and dark glasses. A few yards inside the forest, they blended so well with the fir trees against which they leant as to be almost invisible.

They heard clearly the fanfare of horns warning of the ski-train's departure from Bretaye above them. It was the signal they were awaiting. Gunther looked at his watch.

'Maidment should be leaving now, if he's on time,' he said. 'We ought to get ready for him.'

Trina nodded, as she pulled a ski-mask up to cover her mouth and nose, and render herself completely unrecognizable. Though he had objected that such precautions were unnecessary, Gunther did the same.

A party of four young people, probably students, came down the *piste* in file. Their leader, ski-ing a little too fast, lost control on a turn, and slid unceremoniously into a snow-drift. There was confusion as the others halted and pulled him out, laughing at his mishap. Trina and Gunther drew back into the trees. If Maidment appeared at this moment it would be awkward for him to ski into the forest and join them, without arousing curiosity.

'*Schnell! Schnell! Schnell!*' Gunther muttered as the young

81

party indulged in some raucous horseplay. Then they were on their way, and he relaxed. 'Where the hell is Maidment?' he demanded.

'Coming right now, I think.'

Trina pointed to a figure who was taking the turn wide and easily, leaning his body into the bend. The icy snow of the *piste* crunched under his skis as he came to an abrupt halt opposite them. Then, after a quick glance behind him, he moved across the slope. He reached them before anyone else appeared on the run, and they drew him deeper into the trees.

'Mr Maidment?'

Maidment took his time removing his skis and thrusting them into the snow. 'Who else would be here to meet *you*?' He was making no concessions to politeness.

Trina laughed. 'Push up your goggles, please, and pull down your mask. I want to see your face.'

Maidment hesitated, then did as he was told. This, presumably, was Mrs Carpenter – he was almost sure that he recognized the voice – but he would never be able to identify her positively. The ski clothes and equipment were an effective disguise.

'You know what I want,' Maidment said abruptly. 'My son! What the hell do *you* want?'

'Just a little help. A little co-operation.' Trina studied him. Not particularly handsome, she thought, but attractive, with a good, firm mouth. He looked the sort of man on whom one could depend and, even in these strange circumstances, he showed no outward sign of fear – at least not for himself. She nodded her satisfaction. 'How are your nerves, Mr Maidment?'

Maidment stared at her. 'In God's name, what have my nerves got to do with it? They're strained, Mrs Carpenter, quite naturally. What the hell do you expect? You've kidnapped my son. You're keeping him a prisoner – a kind of hostage, I suppose. Why? For God's sake, why?'

'You've said it yourself, Mr Maidment. He's a hostage – to ensure that you do as we ask.'

'But why me? Why pick on me and my son?'

'You really want to know? I should have thought you might have guessed. You drive regularly between France and Switzerland in a car with consular – effectively diplomatic – licence plates. You're well-known at the border, and the tightened security hardly bothers you. That's why we've chosen you, Mr Maidment.'

'You're perfect,' Gunther added. 'Absolutely perfect for our purpose.'

'And what's that, Mr – er – Carpenter?'

Trina threw back her head and laughed aloud. 'Mr Carpenter!' she repeated. 'Mr and Mrs Carpenter! What an idea!'

Maidment saw the man's jaw tighten. Obviously he failed to appreciate the joke, if joke it was. The girl was certainly amused. Then she sobered, became businesslike. It was cold under the trees, and stupid to waste time.

'Mr Maidment,' she said, 'tomorrow when you go to Annecy you're to stop at the first *Aire de service* – the only service area you pass before you get to the Annecy turn-off. You must know it – it's a "Total" station called Groisy, going south – and the equivalent on the northbound carriageway is an "Elf" station called Les Crets Blancs. Anyway, arrive at Groisy about ten, go in and have coffee for just half an hour, but leave the keys of your Jaguar in the glove compartment. When you come out you'll find a different car – a Peugeot – in its place. Use that car till Monday evening. Then stop at Les Crets Blancs at six o'clock on your way home and exchange it for your Jaguar in the same way. Is that clear?'

'Perfectly. I take it you'll have put in my car whatever it is you want me to smuggle into Switzerland.'

'Correct, Mr Maidment, so make sure you don't have any trouble at the frontier.'

'And what is it? Counterfeit money? Stolen goods?

83

Drugs?'

'That's no business of yours, and I advise you not to investigate. Just drive back to your house, garage your car, but leave your car and garage unlocked. Your car will be removed and returned later. Do you understand?'

'I must know what I'm carrying. Is it drugs?' Maidment persisted. He didn't really care; with Derek's life at stake he was prepared to smuggle anything. But the more they talked, the better chance he had of learning something that might prove useful later. It was the only form of insurance he could claim, and he knew only too well how pathetic it was. 'Heroin?' he demanded, when there was no answer.

The girl remained silent, but her companion's reaction was unexpected; it was his turn to hint at some obscure joke. 'Heroin?' he said. 'Big H? Horse? What you mean, chum, is little –'

'*Halt das Mahl!* Shut up!' Trina swung round savagely on Gunther.

For a lengthening minute the silence between them was almost tangible. Then, somewhere deeper in the forest, a bough creaked under its weight of snow. From the ice rink far below in Villars rose the sound of music, thin and unreal in the cold air. A fir cone fell at Maidment's feet.

Ignoring Gunther, Trina said, 'Mr Maidment, those are your instructions. Follow them. Don't try to play any tricks, or you'll never see your son alive again. But do as you've been told and he'll be free by the end of next week.'

'I'll do as you say,' Maidment said slowly.

Trina was already turning away and clumping through the trees. Gunther followed her. Maidment watched them till they were out of sight. He found himself breathing hard, as if he'd run a mile. The end of next week, he thought, and wondered if he dare believe the woman. Once Derek was released he could go to the authorities. No one would blame him for his silence. But what could he tell them? He knew so little about his enemies, and if they were as confident as they seemed . . .

Sighing, Maidment pulled his skis from the snow and carried them back to the *piste*. A couple swept by as he was snapping them on, but they paid him no attention; if they thought about him at all, they probably assumed that he had gone into the trees to relieve himself. He drove in his poles and set off down the rest of the ski-run to Villars. He skied automatically, but carefully. The mist was slowly thickening, and he didn't want an accident. A broken arm or a leg would be the last straw; he didn't think that Mrs Carpenter would accept such an excuse for him not playing the role she had planned for him.

In the tension of the encounter in the forest Maidment had totally forgotten Peter Bingham, and he was surprised to find his friend waiting at the bottom of the run. Bingham was a tall man with dark, curly hair, and his long face was rueful. He was full of apologies.

'Rory, I really am most terribly sorry. What can I say? I've let you down.'

'It doesn't matter. They were too clever for me, anyway.'

Bingham hid his dismay. It was not his fault that he had arrived in Villars so late. There had been an accident just ahead of him on the Autoroute from Berne; an articulated lorry had jack-knifed across the whole of the southbound road. First he had been held up, then the traffic had been diverted. He had thought it best to wait for Maidment at their rendezvous, rather than risk missing him altogether.

Nevertheless, he wouldn't have minded if Maidment had blamed him. It was his friend's appearance that was worrying. He had never seen Rory look more despairing, not even after the death of his wife. The dead Sarah reminded Bingham of Marie-Louise Grandin.

'Rory, is something wrong with Marie-Louise?'

'Marie-Louise?' Maidment sounded vaguely puzzled.

'Come along,' Bingham said. 'I've a flask in my car. We could both do with a drink.'

'It's Derek, not Marie-Louise,' Maidment said finally, as they set off together. He told Bingham everything, holding nothing back, and was surprised at how little there was to tell.

Peter Bingham thought for a moment, and finally summed it up. 'It's a classic situation, I'm afraid,' he said. 'You really ought to go to the authorities, Rory, but of course I understand. It's Derek's life against God knows what, possibly a parcel of heroine or –' He hesitated. 'You do realize there's no guarantee – none at all – that they'll release Derek, even if you keep your side of the bargain?'

'I know,' Maidment said miserably. 'But my options are limited. What choice have I? I've got to try to save him.'

Nine

Easter Monday, and in England it was two o'clock in the morning. Geoffrey Linton slid quietly out of bed. His mind was unbearably active, and he was afraid his constant tossing and turning as he tried to get comfortable might wake his wife, for once peacefully asleep in the next bed.

The curtains were partly drawn to allow air from the open window to circulate in the room, and the moonlight showed the lines of pain and tiredness etched in Julia's face. Linton smiled at her fondly. He was so glad to have her home, and thankful that seemingly the accident had caused her no lasting harm.

He put on a robe, thrust his feet into an old pair of leather slippers and let himself out of the bedroom. He went down to the kitchen and put on the kettle to make tea. It was one of those occasions when he wished he smoked. Fiddling with a pipe, lighting it, keeping it alight, might have occupied him mentally, if not physically. He felt incredibly tense.

When the tea was ready he took a mug along to his study. He sat at his desk and began to make notes on a tricky problem that had been causing him some bother at the office, but he found he couldn't concentrate. His thoughts were always deflected by this niggling personal worry.

Why was he worrying? He tried to argue with himself. Julia had had a bad time, but she had been lucky; she would soon be fit again. He found himself imagining what might have been – Julia dead or paralysed, unthinkably condemned to a wheelchair for the rest of her life. He shook his head as his thoughts turned to Derek. The boy had been lucky, too –

unhurt and now safe with his father. True, Julia's car was a write-off, but that was trivial; in any case, the insurance would pay. Why not forget the incident?

He knew the answer to that question, but it wasn't one he wanted to accept. He was afraid – for himself and for Julia; thank God his sons were both abroad. On the surface his doubts were absurd, but the fact that Special Branch had identified the two men as part of an international terrorist group was difficult to shrug off. It had been enough to keep him awake at nights while he and the police waited for the next move – the threatening letter or phone call.

'See what we've done already. We'll do it again, and worse, unless . . .' Unless, what? 'Unless you persuade the Home Secretary to release a certain prisoner,' perhaps. But there had been no such letter, no such call, and surely by now the time for an approach of this sort was past. Even the authorities were beginning to relax their initial vigilance.

Geoffrey Linton sighed, finished his mug of tea, returned it neatly to its place in the kitchen and went back to bed. Julia was still fast asleep, but it was some time before Linton slept. It was no use telling himself again and again that he was being fanciful, that even if there had ever been an intended plot against himself and his family, the danger was over. He remained oppressed by a sense that something was very wrong.

★

Not so many miles away, though in a different English county, Nana Smith was also unable to sleep. It was pain that kept her awake, and the pills the doctors had prescribed with their reassuring smiles were no damned use. Like Linton, she got up, and began to prowl about her bedroom.

The pain came in waves, making her giddy and nauseous in turn. Once or twice she had to cling to the bed rail until the worst of the agony subsided. The doctors had subjected her to a lot of tests and told her that she must hold herself ready to come into hospital for an operation. They had said it would be soon, but they had refused to say when. But now her condition seemed to have worsened; she was sweating heavily and she was frightened. It was no longer a question of being summoned to hospital without warning. To judge from the acuteness of the pain, she might collapse and die at any time, with the boy locked in his attic room, and no means of letting Trina know. It wasn't that she was afraid of death – she had a good idea of what the doctors had been keeping from her, and at seventy-five she could scarcely hope for many more years. But she didn't want to die with a task half completed.

Perhaps she had been stupid not to tell Trina of her situation. She had argued that Trina would find it difficult to make alternative arrangements for the boy, and for the house, but she was no fool. She appreciated that her desire not to let Trina down was at least partly a cloak for an old woman's vanity.

Nana Smith sat on the edge of her bed, smoothing her flannel nightdress over her knees, and wondered what she should do. She did have a telephone number for extreme emergencies, but she had never had occasion to use it. Now, as she hesitated, the pain began to ease. The relief was enormous and, after a while, when it didn't return, she decided to take no action, at least for the time being.

If she continued to feel better, she thought, she would make a cake for the boy's birthday on Tuesday. He had told her he usually had lots of presents but there wouldn't be much for him this year, poor child; only a small box of chocolate mints and, if she felt up to it, a cake. She must make him a cake.

Smiling to herself, Nana Smith climbed back into bed and pulled up the duvet. Soon she slept.

★

In Switzerland it was five o'clock on Easter Monday morning. Trina Hansen had read till two, and since then had dozed fitfully. She hadn't expected to sleep. Her mind was far too active as again and again she reviewed the day ahead, searching for some detail she had missed, anything that could have been foreseen, but if unforeseen might bring disaster.

She slid out of bed. It was essential to relax and get more rest, even if she was unable to sleep. She couldn't afford to be dull-witted today, of all days. Slipping on a robe she left her room in search of Gunther.

Arndt Gunther woke from a nightmare, disturbed by the gentle but persistent tapping at his door. For a moment he couldn't remember his whereabouts, but as he switched on the bedside light and revealed the hotel room he was at once alert.

'Who's that?' he demanded, going to the door, but not opening it till Trina spoke. He let her in. 'Is something wrong?' he asked anxiously.

'Only that I can't sleep.'

Moving past him into the room Trina let her robe fall apart. She was wearing nothing underneath, and Gunther drew in a quick breath. He felt himself begin to harden and, hurriedly putting the chain back on the door, stripped off his pyjama jacket and ran to the bed where Trina lay, arms and legs wide, waiting for him.

The number of times that Trina Hansen had come to Arndt Gunther's bed could be counted on one hand. Always it had been at her initiative. Always Gunther had been used; his only proposition had been treated with such contempt that he had never repeated it. And always their encounters had followed the same pattern, a swift, violent coupling, followed by a slow languorous love-making – if one could call it that – during which Trina kept her eyes shut and fantasized that Gunther was Horst Zabel. She didn't pretend otherwise.

Finally satisfied, Trina went into the bathroom, leaving Gunther to indulge in his own dreams. There had been a coldness between them since the meeting with Maidment on Friday. Trina had been furiously angry with him and, ski-ing back to Les Chaux, had accused him of putting them all at risk with his stupid joke about 'Big H'. He was glad at least that difference seemed to be resolved. Today was going to be tense enough, without any feelings of recrimination in the air. By tonight, he thought, he could be in gaol, or even dead. Or he might be drinking champagne with Trina as a celebration. But there was a long way to go before either event.

Trina's thoughts had clearly been running on the same lines. When she returned to the bedroom, her robe firmly tied around her, she was businesslike. 'You've quite a lot of driving to do today, Arndt,' she said, 'and traffic could be heavy. You'd better think about getting up.'

'Not to worry. I'll be where I'm needed.' Gunther grinned. He wanted to reassure her, to promise her that the operation would be a success, but he couldn't think what to say. There were still so many imponderables . . .

★

In France, in the Grandins' house on Lac d'Annecy, Rory Maidment slept the sleep of exhaustion. Lying beside him, Marie-Louise watched with love the steady rise and fall of his chest. The tired lines on his face and the fluttering movements of his limbs as he dreamed made her want to weep, though she wasn't a weak woman.

She and Rory had talked far into the night. She had argued with him. She wanted to help, but he was adamant, and finally she had promised – but only that she wouldn't use her car, which might be recognized. She smiled to herself. Rory knew nothing of the motor cycle she hoped to borrow from a neighbour's son.

Her father always rose early, and his first task was to put on the coffee. As soon as Marie-Louise smelt it she got out of bed, leaving Maidment sleeping, and quietly pulled on jeans and a shirt. Denis would have returned to his room to wash and shave, she knew, so it was a good moment to slip out of the house without explanations.

She returned ten minutes later, well pleased. She had been able to borrow the motor bike, and a helmet which would serve as a perfect disguise. Both were safely hidden in an easily available place at the end of the garden.

But she hadn't reckoned on her father's astuteness. 'You've been up to something,' he said, as soon as she came into the kitchen and he'd greeted her.

Marie-Louise waved away the accusation. 'Rory's still asleep,' she said. 'I shan't wake him.'

'Marie-Louise! What is it? I want to know. I have a right to know.' Denis Grandin rarely spoke to his daughter with such firmness. 'You are planning something.'

'It's all right, Papa,' she said at once, eager to reassure him. 'I don't intend to do anything dangerous. I've borrowed Pierre's motor bike. I'm just going to follow Rory this evening and watch to see who returns his car at the *Aire de service* at Les Crets Blancs. If – if after today little Derek isn't released quickly, the more we know about these people the better. You must appreciate that, Papa.'

'Of course, yes. But . . . Does Rory know what you're planning?'

'No, and you mustn't tell him. He said I wasn't to involve myself, more than I'm already involved. After all, it's known I'm his girlfriend, but that's all. He wants it to stay like that. No active involvement – those were his words. But I want to help him, Papa. I can't let myself be shut out from something so important to him.'

Denis Grandin nodded. 'No,' he said reluctantly, 'I suppose you can't, *chérie*. But please – for my sake – take care.'

★

It was not a happy day for anyone concerned. For Rory

Maidment the waiting was intolerable, and he was thankful when the time came for him to say goodbye, to kiss Marie-Louise and wring Denis Grandin's hand. Kind and understanding as they both were, in his present state he preferred to be alone – and now, at least, there was to be some action.

Arndt Gunther, sitting in his BMW which he had parked unobtrusively on the shoulder at the end of the road that led to the Grandins' house, saw Maidment leave and noted with satisfaction that he was keeping to schedule. The satisfaction, however, was short-lived. He was about to draw out and follow Maidment at a discreet distance when he spotted what he took to be a youth on a motor bike who looked as if he might have the same objective.

Gunther told himself not to jump to conclusions; the motor-cyclist could be a coincidence, for the Grandins' road was not entirely unfrequented. But his suspicions had been aroused, and he trusted his instinct. Frowning heavily he set off in pursuit of both Maidment in the Peugeot and the unknown on the motor bike.

It was at the first set of traffic lights that Gunther's misgivings were confirmed. The accepted behaviour for anyone on a motor cycle caught in traffic is to edge forward between vehicles until he heads the jam and is in position to zoom off immediately the lights change. If the youth had done that he would have found himself alongside Maidment. Instead, he seemingly took care to tuck himself in behind a convenient van.

That was enough for Gunther. He could be wrong, but he was not about to take any risks. As soon as possible he would arrange a little accident for the motor bike and its rider. Meanwhile, overtaking the car in front of him, he decreased the distance between them. When the opportunity came he was ready, directly behind the bike, with no one too close behind him and a bend in the road ahead.

As they rounded the bend Gunther suddenly accelerated, drew level with the motor bike and cut in viciously, sideswiping it. Marie-Louise had no chance. The attack was completely unexpected, and even if she had been a more experienced rider there was nothing she could have done to save herself. The bike slid from under her, the ground came up and hit her, and thankfully she blacked out.

Smiling grimly, Gunther at once accelerated, passing a truck and another car before easing up to the rear of Maidment's Peugeot. Maidment, oblivious of the drama that had been played out behind him, was driving at a steady speed. His immediate purpose was to collect his own car at Les Crets Blancs, drive it back to Switzerland and into his garage. Then the plan he had agreed with Peter Bingham would go into action.

As on the outward journey, the change-over in the *Aire de service* worked smoothly. Watched by Gunther, Maidment parked the Peugeot and set off in search of the prescribed cup of coffee. Fifteen minutes later his Jaguar was driven into the parking lot. The driver located the Peugeot without difficulty, and made the change; later, of course, the Peugeot would be abandoned.

Maidment had been allowed thirty minutes, and he re-appeared on the dot. Without bothering to check if anyone was taking any notice of him he went directly to his Jag, got in and drove off – ostensibly a consular officer stationed in Switzerland, who had been to France for the Easter vacation.

Maidment had been instructed to drive as fast as he could when he left Les Crets Blancs, but the holiday weekend was coming to a close and traffic was heavy. By the time he reached the border near Annemasse there was a long tail-back of vehicles. And Gunther, to his annoyance, found that he was separated from Maidment by several cars.

Gunther sat in the queue and fumed. The build-up of traffic, which had been judged an advantage, was turning out to be disadvantageous because, in spite of the congestion and the growing impatience of the travellers, some of them families with small and fractious children, few concessions were being made by the authorities. Vehicles were being searched, papers and passengers carefully scrutinized. Holiday weekend or not, the officials seemed determined to do their duty. Gunther could guess why.

Then it came to Maidment's turn. Recognized because of his frequent border-crossing, and out of respect for his consular status, his papers were given a more cursory inspection. But the boot of the car, in which he'd flung a bag and a raincoat to distract curious eyes from the modification, was for once opened. As the officer glanced in Maidment began to sweat.

A minute later, the lid of the boot was slammed shut. The officer grinned. '*Ça va, monsieur*,' he said cheerfully, waving Maidment on. To his enormous relief – and that of Gunther, whose own car was being thoroughly examined – Rory Maidment drove slowly into Switzerland. Neither of them could believe that it had been so simple.

Ten

From Peter Bingham's point of view Geneva's old town had one great advantage: the twists and turns of its narrow streets gave plenty of cover. There were many places – entrances or doorways – where a man could wait without drawing undue attention to himself, seeing but unseen. An alley leading from the Rue de Haut not far from the stone archway that gave access to the cobbled courtyard of Maidment's house was one such place.

Bingham was there now, waiting for Maidment – and worried. All his professional instincts told him that they were crazy to take on the kidnappers alone. Still, he had given his word to Rory, and the two of them had made their plans as carefully as possible the previous Friday. Bingham would return to Berne, but on Monday he would rent a car without diplomatic plates, drive to Geneva and take up his position off the Rue de Haut in readiness for Maidment's return from Annecy that evening. He would continue to wait and watch till Maidment's Jaguar was collected from its garage when, with any luck, he would be able to follow it to its eventual destination. It was really a job for three or four cars and a team of experts, he reflected, but he must just do the best he could.

The car he had rented, with some difficulty on an Easter weekend, was an inconspicuous Renault, and it was now parked a little way down the street. Bingham shifted from one foot to another, resisting the temptation to look at his watch yet again. Unless something had gone wrong, either in the *Aire de service* at Les Crets Blancs or, more likely, at the

Swiss frontier, Maidment should be arriving at any moment.

A couple turned into the alley and glanced at Bingham without curiosity, probably assuming he was waiting for a girl. They had scarcely passed when Bingham saw the Jaguar drive by, brake sharply and turn into the courtyard. He sighed with relief. At least there had been no trouble at the border. And, as the minutes went by and no car decided to park, no pedestrian showed any inclination to linger, Bingham grew confident that no one was close on Maidment's tail.

This was good news. If Maidment were to carry out his part of the plan, it was now that he needed time. Bingham wished he could have been with him. Watching the road for anything that might imply a threat, he pictured Maidment setting to work in the garage, and willed him to hurry. He regretted that they had been unable to devise some means of communication, but – even with his connections – it had proved impossible to acquire 'walkie-talkies' or anything of that kind in the short time available.

Before he had left the house on Saturday, Maidment had put ready and available all the tools he would need to open the compartment in the Jaguar's boot and examine its contents – screwdrivers, a powerful hand lamp, a camera and even a plastic bag in case it was possible to take some sort of sample. He had, he hoped, thought of everything.

Nevertheless, the task was not simple, especially under stress. The need for speed warred with the need to take care. Against all his instructions, he had taken the precaution of locking the garage door from the inside, but this would not help for long if he were too slow and whoever was to collect the car arrived before he was finished. On the other hand, if he failed to take adequate care he could leave evidence of his tampering. Already a screwdriver had slipped and there was a nasty betraying mark on the false panel.

Partly from nerves, and partly because it was hot and airless in the garage, even with the door to the house open,

97

Maidment was sweating heavily, which didn't help. His hand was inclined to slip, and he became more and more conscious of his clumsiness. He began to wonder if his efforts were worthwhile. Probably all he would find would be a collection of carefully-packaged parcels, and photographing these would prove nothing. He didn't think he dared pierce one in order to examine its contents; any such attempt would arouse immediate suspicion. The best he could hope for was that one of the parcels had split open.

Constantly, at the back of his mind, was the thought of Derek. Whatever he was doing, he was doing for Derek's sake. The boy came first. If Derek was returned to him safe and well. . . But his doubts were growing. The kidnapping of a multi-millionaire's son could be resolved by payment. A political hi-jacking could always be ended *in extremis* by the satisfaction of the hi-jacker's demands.

This case was quite different. Payment for Derek's well-being was being made by a kind of service – a service abhorrent in itself, but necessary in the circumstances. Yet when that service was completed, what was to prevent Mrs Carpenter and her colleagues from asking – demanding – that it should be repeated? As long as the boy was in their hands, they held a trump card, and Maidment had little doubt they'd have no hesitation in playing it.

There was a sound in the courtyard, and Maidment froze. He had been on the point of lifting out the false partition. He turned slowly towards the garage door and waited, his mouth dry, for signs that someone was attempting to open it.

Nothing happened, except that the sound from outside was repeated. Then there was a flurry of movement and a cat mewed. Silently swearing at the unnecessary delay, Maidment turned back to the car. Quickly he lifted out the partition and, seizing the hand lamp, illuminated the compartment.

For a moment he stared in disbelief, his jaw dropping. Then, almost in a trance, he arranged the lamp and picked up the camera. He and Bingham had considered every possibility, or thought they had. Heroin, cocaine, LSD or some similar substance had been their favourite choices, but there had been a string of alternatives – weapons, forged notes, money to be laundered, even stolen paintings or illicitly exported *objets d'art*. What had not crossed their minds was that the cargo might be human. HA!

The man was small, but even so, with his knees drawn up tight against his chest and, except for his face, totally encased in foam rubber, he only just fitted into the space available. Maidment wouldn't have believed it possible. Nevertheless, here indeed was a man, obviously heavily sedated, but alive, his breathing shallow but steady.

And Maidment recognized him. In fact, there were few people with access to the Western media who wouldn't have known him. In the last few weeks his features had been plastered over every newspaper, appeared on every television screen, been billed at every frontier post or police station or *gendarmerie* or *Politzeiwache* or *questura* in Europe. This was the man who had almost killed the President of France, and was wanted for so many other successful assassinations. The man was a cold-blooded murderer, though he would probably call himself a 'freedom fighter' or some such euphemism.

Rory Maidment had to steady himself before he could take any photographs. His discovery put a new complexion on the situation. The death of the *garagiste* had demonstrated that he was dealing with a gang who would not hesitate to kill, but he hadn't realized that the stakes were so very high. He knew now that, in spite of the promises he had received, Derek's chances of survival were negligible, and that what he should do was summon the authorities at once. But he couldn't bring himself to face this fact, or to act on it.

Automatically he completed his photography, laid aside the camera, and set to work closing the compartment. He worked more rapidly now that he knew the worst. Somehow the task seemed simpler, and he was soon finished. He cleared away all signs of what he had been doing, remembered to unlock the garage door, and went into the house, still undecided about what action to take.

★

Maidment need not have hurried. It was another twenty minutes before Peter Bingham saw a blue BMW drop off its passenger, who went swiftly through the archway that led to Maidment's house. The BMW parked further along the road. Bingham made no move.

He had caught only a glimpse of what looked like an attractive girl driving the BMW, and a nondescript man entering the arch. He guessed they were the couple that Maidment had met in the pine forest below Bretaye – Mr and Mrs Carpenter, if by any unlikely chance these were their real names – but, like Maidment, he would have been unable to provide an adequate description of either of them. He continued to wait, his excitement rising.

This time there was only a short pause. Soon the Jaguar drove out and turned to the left, away from him. The BMW allowed it to pass, then followed. Bingham ran to his Renault, fortunately facing in the right direction, flung himself in and set off in pursuit. This, he knew, was a tricky moment. If he lost them, he'd have failed Rory Maidment, and Derek. Equally, if his attempts at tailing the cars were noticed, Derek's life could be endangered.

Luck was with him. The fact that he had two cars to follow helped. He could easily have lost the Jaguar, but he saw the BMW turn off the Rue de Haut and, closing up on it, knew that in spite of the winding streets, he was in touch with his quarries, at least for the moment.

They were now out of the old town, and traffic was heavier, especially on this Monday night, at the end of the holiday. This was an advantage on the wide Pont du Mont-Blanc and along the quais towards the Autoroute to Lausanne, for Bingham could conceal himself amongst the other vehicles. Trina Hansen was doing her best to drive protectively behind the Jaguar, but she didn't immediately spot the Renault. The delays at the border had caused Gunther to be late at their rendezvous, and she had been almost sick with anxiety. The relief she had felt when he finally arrived and reported that Maidment had crossed safely into Switzerland with his precious cargo was still distracting her.

But once they left the Autoroute beyond Nyon, and began to climb along steep and winding minor roads into the hills north of Lac Léman, it was impossible not to notice the Renault. There was nothing to suggest it was following them, but Trina took evasive action. At the first opportunity she blinked her headlights and turned off into a rutted lane. Gunther, she knew, would have seen her in his rear-view mirror, and understood the warning.

Peter Bingham had no choice. He ignored the BMW and followed the Jag, though the blue car's unexpected turn had him worried. He was not surprised when some minutes later he saw the car reappear behind him, but he felt a shiver of fear.

Three or four kilometres further on, rounding a bend, Bingham realized that the Jaguar was no longer ahead of him. But his eye had caught sight of a neat signboard beside the road. Its silver lettering on a dark blue background announced the presence of the Clinique de la Rocque, a thousand metres down a side turning. Bingham drove straight on, aware that the BMW was still on his tail.

He was half afraid the car might force him to stop or try to drive him off the road, but it kept its distance, the driver unsure, Bingham guessed, as to whether or not he posed a threat. Then he had a stroke of luck. He came upon a small inn that advertised itself as a restaurant and, from the number of cars outside, was well patronized. He thankfully drove in. Here was a legitimate excuse for his trip from

Geneva.

As he got out of the Renault, the BMW went past, but Bingham took no chances. He went into the inn and, watching the road through a window, asked for a table. The restaurant was crowded and he hoped to be refused, but a place was found for him. He ordered food and wine, though two minutes later he couldn't have said what he was to eat and drink. But he had the satisfaction of seeing the BMW return and drive past the inn without stopping.

★

As time went by Rory Maidment found himself still unable to make up his mind. He despised himself for his vacillation, but he told himself that the effects of any action on Derek must be his primary consideration. Weakly he decided to wait, in the forlorn hope that Peter Bingham would return with information that might help towards a decision.

When the phone rang he leapt for it, spilling the drink he had just poured. 'Yes. Maidment here.'

'Rory, it's Peter. I can't talk now, but all's well and I'll be back as soon as I can. I may be some time. I've got to eat a damned dinner first, and I'm quite a way from Geneva.'

Dinner? In the background Maidment heard the murmur of voices, the rattle of crockery, the sound of cutlery on china, then a sudden searing roar that caused a lull in the conversation. Maidment experienced a moment of panic before he realized what was happening; then he pictured the flame leaping from the pan as the brandy was ignited over a Steak Diane. There was no doubt that Peter was in a restaurant. But why? How?

'Rory! Are you all right?'

'Yes. Sorry, Peter. I don't understand, but I – I'll see you later. As soon as you can, though. I've got news.'

'Me too.'

'Okay. But for God's sake, take care.'

102

'That's exactly why I'm here. Don't worry.'

Easy to say, Maidment thought bitterly as he mopped up the spilt whisky and gave himself another drink. But how could he not worry?

Maidment never knew how he survived the hours that followed. There was no question of bed. He was unwilling to drink too much, in case he needed all his wits the next day. He paced between his chair and the windows overlooking the courtyard. He found a bundle of old newspapers and magazines in the kitchen, stacked ready for the garbage collection, and forced himself to look through them for anything he might learn about the man he'd found. There was a lot of material, some of it contradictory, none of it adding anything really useful to what he knew already.

In fact, little was known about the assassin; the only photograph had been taken in the Place de l'Opéra. His nationality and name remained untraced, though there was much speculation. He was said to be part German, part Turkish, part Ukrainian. His employers, if he had any, were unspecified, though there seemed no reason to doubt the belief of the pundits that he was a member of – possibly the leader of – some terrorist group which operated to destabilize the Western democracies.

It was the early hours before Maidment heard a car drive into the courtyard. He ran to the window, careful not to disturb the curtains, and peered out. The Jaguar had been returned, but its driver was in a hurry; he left the car standing in front of the garage and walked briskly from the courtyard. Even in the dim light Maidment was sure it was the same man -- the man who had collected the car, the man he had met with Mrs Carpenter.

Forcing himself to delay for five minutes, Maidment went out and drove the car into the garage. He pulled down the garage door, and opened the car's boot. From the bits of foam rubber on the floor it was clear that the compartment had been exposed in haste, so as to free the sedated man as rapidly as possible. No attempt had been made to hide what had been done, though there was no indication that the foam rubber had protected a human passenger.

Among the debris was a large piece of paper on which someone had scribbled in capital letters, 'DEREK WILL PHONE TOMORROW 1900 HOURS'. Rory Maidment looked at it for some time before he picked it up between two fingers. He knew his freedom of action was still inhibited, and he was still staring at the paper when Peter Bingham arrived.

Eleven

Derek Maidment woke early. He got out of bed and went to the window, where he curled himself up on its seat. The sun was pale, but promised warmth later, and the birds were singing bravely. The garden, which by now he knew well, looked mysterious and inviting. At least it seemed as if the weather was going to be lovely for his tenth birthday.

Derek bit his bottom lip hard. His eyes had grown misty, but he blinked away the moisture. He mustn't cry, not today of all days. With any luck Nana Smith would let him go into the garden to play. She knew it was his birthday, and he'd told her how much attention his family paid to such celebrations; maybe she had even planned some treat for him.

But when she came up to unlock the door of his room, Nana Smith seemed especially dour and unsmiling. She asked him if he'd washed and cleaned his teeth and, when he nodded, told him to come to breakfast at once. She made no reference to his birthday, and he wondered if she'd forgotten, or if she was feeling ill again; she had been unable to conceal from him all her bouts of pain. Miserably he followed the old woman down the stairs.

His delight was thus the greater when, on entering the kitchen, he saw the table where his place was laid. Nana Smith hadn't forgotten! There were roses in a bowl, an exciting-looking packet and, propped against his boiled egg which was keeping warm under its little knitted cosy, was a birthday card. It was a cat, cut out of black cardboard, with the greetings written in yellow crayon. Derek guessed that Nana Smith had made it for him herself, but that in some way made it all the better.

'Thank you. Thank you,' he said. He wrapped his arms around her waist, which was almost as high as he could reach, and hugged her. 'Thank you, Nana.'

'It's not much. Just some chocolates and a card. Nothing to make a fuss about.' She spoke gruffly, turning hastily away from him. 'You'd have been getting a lot more, I dare say, if you'd not been here.'

'Yes.' Derek didn't want to think of what might have been. Sitting down at the table, he opened the packet and found the chocolate mints, then started on his egg.

Nana Smith watched him with something akin to affection. 'I've a piece of good news for you, too, Derek. You're going to be allowed to speak to your father again this evening.'

Derek looked up from his breakfast, but made no reply. His last conversation with his father hadn't been particularly encouraging. He wasn't sure that he wanted to face another one like it, even on his birthday.

'Aren't you pleased?' Nana Smith asked at last.

'Yes, of course,' Derek said, but without conviction.

★

Rory Maidment's feelings were equally ambivalent. He and Peter Bingham had argued far into the night. Bingham had maintained that their duty was now clear – the discovery of the wanted man and his apparent hide-out must put an end to equivocation and the authorities must be informed no matter what the cost. He had appealed to Maidment to let him handle the matter 'through his channels', as he put it, and guaranteed the utmost secrecy.

But Maidment had remained adamant, and after a good deal of heart-searching, Bingham had allowed himself to be persuaded into an uneasy compromise, which satisfied neither of them.

'I've done everything they asked,' Maidment had said. 'This Mrs Carpenter promised that, if I did, they'd free Derek by the end of the week. I realize her promise probably isn't worth a damn, but they have kept their word in the past – and I've got to go on hoping. Please agree to leave it at least till Saturday, and then we can reconsider. Let's face it, Peter, after going to such trouble to get here, the man's almost certainly not going to try to leave Switzerland before the weekend.'

'All right, I understand.' Bingham had swallowed what could have been a sigh. All his sympathies were with Maidment – and with Derek. The boy was his godson and he was very fond of him.

But his every instinct rebelled against keeping the new-found and all-important evidence to himself. Counter-intelligence and security were important aspects of his job, and he knew more about terrorism than most people. He was aware of the willingness of people in Rory's situation to grasp at every straw, their overwhelming desire to avoid annoying their blackmailers, even sometimes anger at their helpers.

But never before had he been involved personally. The present situation was teaching him a lot, Bingham thought grimly, but it was a lesson he could do without. He slept little during what remained of the night, though a point did occur to him before he finally dropped into a restless doze.

'Rory,' he said, as he was preparing to leave for Berne the next morning, 'I've remembered something. You know you told me how furious Mrs Carpenter was when the guy with her made some crack about "little horse"?'

'Yes. I thought they were talking about heroin, but clearly they weren't.'

'I've got an idea about that. I think you may have misheard, Rory. He didn't say "little horse", but "little Horst". It was a play on words that made him laugh, though she was not amused.'

'So what? Is that important?'

'Probably not, but it could be. Some time ago there was a well-known terrorist called Horst Zabel – well-known in security circles, I mean, not to the general public. He's not been heard of for months, as far as I know, but he just might be our man. He was said to have an English mistress.'

'Mrs Carpenter?'

'Could be.'

Maidment grinned ruefully. He was grateful to Bingham for agreeing to suppress his professional instincts temporarily, but he couldn't see how putting a name to the man would help Derek. In any event, they were building an identification on the slimmest foundations. 'I'll keep in touch,' he said.

'Yes,' Bingham said sharply. 'Let me know at once if there are any developments. And I'll be back here, on duty, either at the end of the week or the beginning of next.' He didn't say what duty, but both of them knew that, unless the position had been resolved by then, vital decisions would have to be faced.

'Well, you've a key if I'm out or at the office and you want to get into the house.'

'Yes. Thanks, Rory. Goodbye for now. And, as I said, keep in touch.'

This parting conversation did little to relax Maidment, but when Bingham had gone he made himself another cup of coffee and considered the day ahead. He had a good many hours to occupy until the evening which, if the past routine were followed, would bring a call from the woman with the deep voice, Nana Smith, who would let him speak to Derek. But he had no wish to stay in the house; Madame Bichaud, who cleaned for him, came in on Tuesdays, and a conversation with her would involve even more unnecessary lies.

With a last glance at Peter Bingham's portrait of Derek and Sarah – something he caught himself looking at more and more often these days – Maidment went to get his car. Officially he was still on leave but, for want of anything better to do, he had decided to go into the office.

He was greeted without surprise, but with some reservations. Several colleagues asked if he had had a good Easter, and how was his son; to all such queries he answered, 'Fine, thanks.' No one inquired whether he'd been to England to visit Derek or, if not, how he'd spent his time. Young Jean Rodway, his secretary, watched him surreptitiously, and jumped to satisfy any request.

'He looks ill to me,' she confided to a friend over lunch. 'He's quite grey under that tan of his, and he's got dark circles round his eyes.'

'Sounds most unattractive.' The friend refused to be impressed. 'He's probably had a dirty weekend with his girl, or he's been on a binge.'

'No. He's worried about something, I'm sure.'

Maidment would have been surprised at the interest he was creating, but he remained unaware of it. Forcing himself to concentrate, he became immersed in his work; the Consulate was not so overstaffed that the paper didn't pile up, even over a holiday. The telephone startled him.

'Maidment!' he snapped.

'Rory? It's Denis Grandin here.'

'Denis?' Maidment felt a frisson of fear, and licked his suddenly dry lips. He tried to swallow, but there was no saliva in his mouth. 'Are you all right?'

'I am, yes. But not Marie-Louise, I regret to say.'

'Marie-Louise! What's happened?'

Denis Grandin explained. Marie-Louise had been seen, pinned under a motor cycle by the side of the road, by the first car that passed after the incident. Fortunately for her, the driver was a businessman with a telephone in his car. He made no attempt to move her, but immediately phoned for help. It was not many minutes before she was rushed to hospital. She had been able to talk, and had told Denis how she had been forced off the road by a blue BMW with Swiss licence plates while following Maidment in his rented

Renault.

'God! How bad is she?'

'There are various minor injuries. Shock. Concussion. But the most serious thing is a broken pelvis.'

'Damn it all! Why did she take such a chance? I told her not to get involved. She said she wouldn't follow me.'

'She wanted to help you. Which is why I'm phoning now. She thought it important you should know about the car.'

'It is. Thank you. Thank her. . . '

The words were inadequate, Maidment knew, but what could he say? That what Marie-Louise had done was useless – worse than useless – that he already knew about the blue BMW, that it would have been better for her, for everyone, if she had stayed at home. That now Mrs Carpenter would be all the more likely to distrust him and, because of this, Derek might suffer.

'Rory, are you there?'

'Yes, I'm here. I was thinking. What about the local police? What do they know?'

'We've told them nothing – not even the description of the car, or that it was Swiss. They're investigating it as a kind of hit and run accident; in their minds it's even possible the driver of the car didn't know what he'd done.'

'Good.'

'And Rory –'

'Yes?'

'Marie-Louise would like to see you. You will come?'

Maidment reacted instinctively. 'No. No, I don't think so.'

'I understand. Other things must take precedence over my daughter.' Denis Grandin spoke coldly and formally.

Glad that Grandin couldn't see him, Maidment gritted his teeth and grimaced as if in pain. 'No, it's not that,' he said slowly. 'Give her all my love. That goes without saying. Tell her it's best if I don't visit her for the moment. Surely you yourself must appreciate that's the wise course to take. The less – close to me she appears, the safer she'll be.'

'Yes.' There was a pause. 'I see. Perhaps you are right, Rory. I'll explain to her. Meanwhile you'll keep in touch?'

'Of course I will. I can't say how sorry I am that this should have happened. I love her very much, you know.'

'Yes, I know. Don't blame yourself. You warned her. Goodbye, Rory. *Dieu te bénit.*'

Thankful that the Consulate was equipped with a modern phone system and that Denis Grandin was using his direct-dial number, so that the chances of the operator overhearing the call were small, Maidment put down the receiver and buried his face in his hands. He stayed like that for several minutes. Then purposefully he lifted his head and returned to his work. When Jean Rodway came in with some papers, he asked casually, 'Jean, do you know anything about the Clinique de la Rocque?'

'No. I've never heard of it, but there are lots of clinics in Switzerland, as you know, sir.'

'It's on the outskirts of Geneva. I guess it's a private hospital of some kind. Go down and look up the odd reference book, will you? Find out what you can about it.'

'Of course, sir.' Jean paused in the doorway.

'It's just that I've had a query from a friend in England, Jean. I want to do what I can to help him.'

More lies, thought Maidment. But it was the sort of question that often had to be answered, and the kind of assignment that Jean enjoyed. She spent part of the afternoon happily in the library. She was efficient and thorough. Not content with all the material she had managed to collect from standard sources, she sought out one of the Consular staff who had recently married a Swiss doctor. She added the extra information she had gleaned from her as a note at the end of the file.

Maidment, who had practically forgotten his inquiry, was surprised at the bulk of paper Jean produced as he was about to leave the office. He smiled his thanks, and put the file in his briefcase to take home. 'Nothing confidential, is there?' he said.

'Oh no, sir. It seems to be rather a well known place.'

'I'll read the file this evening, I promise,' he said.

★

Maidment's first thought on reaching his house was to pour himself a whisky. He was drinking too much, he knew, but alcohol helped to deaden his anxiety. He wondered if he should tell Bingham about Marie-Louise and stretched his hand towards the phone, but then decided against making the call. Peter was back in Berne and busy with his own affairs. In spite of his insistence on being kept informed, it was pointless to bother him about each isolated event.

The phone rang. Too early for Nana Smith and Derek, but all the same Maidment felt his stomach knot. It was a relief to hear Geoffrey Linton's voice. Not that Linton was particularly affable. He had called because Rory hadn't bothered to do so, he indicated. Julia was home and progressing well, but inevitably they'd had a quiet Easter. How was Derek? What sort of holiday had they had? Where had they spent it? Maidment felt that he was being reproached for his disregard of a convalescing Julia, and having his behaviour subjected to cross-examination. He resented it, though he appreciated the reasons for Linton's concern.

To ward off too many questions he talked of ski-ing at Villars with Peter Bingham on Good Friday, and visiting the Grandins at Lac d'Annecy for the rest of the weekend. Continually he used the first person plural, so that Derek was included. He no longer had any conscience about lying to his brother-in-law and he was ready when Linton asked the inevitable.

'Derek's having a good time then? That's splendid.' Geoffrey Linton wasn't usually so hearty. 'Maybe you'd let me have a word with him, Rory. There are still those questions,

112

you know.'

'He's not here. I left him with the Grandins. He was loving it there so much I thought it unfair to bring him back to Geneva, especially as I've got to work this week. And I want Marie-Louise to get to know him well. I'm sure you understand, Geoffrey.' Trying to visualize the expression on Linton's face, Maidment hurried on. 'Geoffrey, I must go. There's someone at the door. Goodbye. My love to you both. I'll phone you soon.'

He put down the instrument and swallowed the rest of his drink. Not long now before he would be speaking to Derek. Mentally he rehearsed what he would say. He knew it would be much harder to lie to the boy than to Geoffrey, but he had no choice. To fill in time, he poured himself another drink, got the file on the Clinique de la Rocque out of his briefcase, and waited for the phone to ring.

The file was not absorbing. He skimmed through the story of the philanthropist who had originally founded the institution some thirty years ago, its modernization, its successes, the important doctors and scientists who were prepared to come and work there. Clearly, its reputation was high. It was difficult to imagine any connection with a group of international terrorists.

He had just reached the note that Jean Rodway had appended at the end of the file when the telephone rang again. Nana Smith was a few minutes early. She gave Maidment the same warning as before, and put Derek on the line.

'Hello, old son, how are you?' Maidment knew his voice sounded false and forced, and he knew that Derek was sensitive enough to know it too.

'All right, thank you, Dad.'

'Have you had a reasonable birthday? Your tenth! Just think, Derek, that puts you in double figures. We must have a wonderful celebration as soon as we get together again. There's a heap of presents waiting for you here.'

'When – when can I come?'

It was the question Maidment had been dreading. He had no wish to raise the boy's hopes, only to have them dashed. 'Next week,' he said finally. 'Perhaps before.'

'I'm due back at school next week.'

God! thought Maidment. Of course! Dates had ceased to mean much to him, and he had completely forgotten about Derek's school. He would have to phone the headmaster and make some excuse. And what was he to say to Geoffrey and Julia, who would be expecting to meet Derek at Heathrow, put him up for the night and take him down to his school the next day?

'Perhaps you can go back late for once.'

'Yes.' The one word, full of the small boy's despair, put an end to the subject.

Father and son talked for another couple of minutes, but the words were meaningless. As on the previous occasion, neither of them was sorry when Nana Smith interrupted them. And yet for both it was dreadful that they had seemingly drifted so far apart.

★

Over the supper that Madame Bichaud had prepared for him and left ready for heating in the oven Maidment re-read the end of the file on the Clinique de la Rocque, including Jean Rodway's final note. This said that, according to a recent rumour, Claude Keller, the Director of the clinic, was about to retire. The generally-accepted reason was ill-health, but some thought his somewhat abrupt departure was due to family problems.

Maidment was not especially interested. Though *Monsieur le directeur* was presumably in an advantageous position if he wanted to admit an assassin to his clinic, it was extremely unlikely that he could do so. Unless there was a general conspiracy among all the doctors and the staff, how could a wanted man, whose face was so well-known, be treated as a patient? But why had he been taken there, if not for treatment?

True, it was believed he had been badly wounded when making his escape after his latest act of terrorism, but that was several weeks ago. Surely treatment would have been easier to arrange in France? Why such a devious plan to get the man to Switzerland? Why take such apparently unnecessary risks?

Maidment had no answers. Some of the questions he had discussed with Bingham the previous night, and they had reached no conclusions. Jean's file hadn't helped much, either. Perhaps because he was tired, perhaps because his mind was so preoccupied, he made the mistake of underestimating the value of Jean Rodway's work.

Twelve

'Don't worry, Claude. The operation will have been successful. You've never had a failure yet. Why should you now?' Marta Braun demanded.

Claude Keller regarded his mistress across his desk in his office at the Clinique de la Rocque, and sighed. She didn't understand, he thought bitterly. How could she? He couldn't tell her how his past had caught up with him.

Claude Keller had been born of German stock in Alsace-Lorraine some sixty-three years ago. A small man with closely-cropped grey hair, a round face and a trim straight-backed figure, he had always kept himself fit, and didn't look his age. He had one physical peculiarity. His heart was on the right rather than the left of his body. This had never inconvenienced him, and indeed he had cause to be grateful for it; instead of being conscripted into the French army at the beginning of World War Two, he had been allowed to pursue his medical studies.

But there had been a price to pay. First, the occupying Germans had compelled him to work in their concentration camps. Then, after the war, when he was beginning to make a name for himself as a plastic surgeon, he had been forced to perform facial operations on several ex-Nazis seeking new lives in South America or elsewhere. The alternative, according to those who approached him, was to be denounced for his earlier work in the camps. He'd had no choice.

How all this had been uncovered, he had no idea. Married to a Swiss, with two children born in Zurich, he had himself been a Swiss citizen for the past thirty years. During that time he had taken such care of his reputation that he had eventually been appointed Director of the prestigious Clinique de la Rocque. His care had even extended to his selection of mistresses – for their suitability and discretion as much as for their looks. There had never been the slightest hint of misconduct, professional or otherwise, in his career. But, in a small closed society like that of Swiss medicine, it had only to be rumoured that he had once worked for the Nazis, even all those years ago, and his career – and with it his world – would disintegrate. And, once he had seen and recognized his latest patient, his fears had redoubled.

'Claude! Did you hear what I said? I asked you why this operation might have turned out badly. You could hardly have failed to make him better-looking.'

Marta Braun frowned at her lover. She was a competent and reasonably attractive woman in her mid thirties, who had been a senior nurse at the clinic for the past five years. She wasn't in love with Keller, but their 'arrangement' suited her well; he was kind, generous and surprisingly good in bed. Her two deepest urges were for money and sex, and he satisfied both.

Nurse Braun hadn't hesitated when Keller had asked her if she was prepared to assist with surgery on someone who was outside the law. The fee, he assured her, would be generous, but when she asked how much, he stated a sum that he knew would have to come from his own bank account. She thought it adequate rather than generous for what was involved, but she didn't quibble. Now she wished she had. Claude Keller was behaving so oddly that he scared her almost as much as the situation in which they found themselves.

'You know as well as I do,' he said. 'The conditions were far from ideal. You were splendid with the anaesthetic and that side went all right – but the risk! First, it's only a short time since the patient was – was badly wounded, and he was still weak. Then, I should really have had more help with the surgery itself. That man Gunther, who made all the arrangements and brought in the patient, and showed me that almost useless little print of what they wanted him to look like – he may have been a medical student once, but he was less use than I expected.'

And you shouldn't have been so nervous yourself, Marta Braun thought; I almost saw your hands shaking. She said, 'Anyway, the patient seems to have borne up remarkably well. He must be as tough as old boots.' She spoke with reluctant admiration; she had been startled, but not as horrified as Keller, when inevitably she'd recognized him.

'Then there's the fact that we didn't use a proper theatre,' Keller continued pursuing his own train of thought. 'I know you did your best, Marta, fitting up my sitting-room, but –'

One of the perquisites of the Director of the clinic was a small apartment – bedroom, sitting-room, bathroom and kitchenette – on the ground floor of the premises, with private access to the grounds. Keller often spent a night there, sometimes with Marta, sometimes alone. It had proved extremely useful, but never so useful as when he had been forced to operate in the strictest secrecy on this terrorist, who was at present occupying his bedroom there.

Marta Braun looked at her watch. 'It's nine o'clock,' she said. 'Time I went and settled our famous – or should it be infamous? – patient for the night. What are you going to do, Claude? Are you going home?'

Keller hadn't thought. He reflected on the events of the last couple of days. Late on Monday night – Easter Monday, of all days – Gunther had arrived with the man under heavy sedation. He'd then disappeared, to return a few hours later. Keller had refused to take the risk of operating until the sedation had worn off and he had had a chance to examine his patient, so the surgery had been postponed till Tuesday morning. That night – last night – the patient had been recovering in the bedroom, Gunther had slept on the sofa in the sitting-room, Marta had snatched a few winks in an armchair with her patient, while he himself had made do with the examination couch in his office. He could hardly do that again without the possibility of arousing comment, when everyone in the clinic was aware he had a perfectly good bed of his own in the same building.

What was more, he hadn't been in touch with his wife since Monday, and though she wasn't a curious woman, it was unusual for him to be on duty two nights in a row. But it was a fair drive to their luxurious villa on the shores of the lake near Lausanne, and his wife might have guests, bridge cronies probably, and he would find it difficult to face them.

He weighed the options. Then, 'Yes, I suppose so,' he said wearily. He felt completely exhausted. 'I'd better go home.'

*

By Thursday Trina Hansen had become impatient. Gunther phoned her regularly from the clinic to keep her posted on Horst Zabel's progress. She knew that he had come through the operation successfully and that everything was fine, as far as it was possible to tell at this point. In fact, they wouldn't know how well Claude Keller had done his job until the moment of truth when the bandages were removed, but the auspices seemed good.

For Trina this was not enough. She wanted to see Zabel herself, to be with him, to speak to him, to touch him. She'd had no physical contact with him for some weeks now, and it irked her that he should be so close and relatively safe, but out of reach. She decided that, when Gunther next phoned, she would insist that he arrange a visit.

'It's not wise, Trina,' Gunther protested.

'Nonsense! I can come in by the private entrance, and the Clinique de la Rocque's a big place. If anyone sees me arriving they'll assume I'm visiting Keller or one of his patients, as indeed I am.'

'I still don't like it, Trina. It's best if we stick to the original plan. No unnecessary movements. I'm sure Horst would

119

agree.'

'I don't care whether you like it or not, Arndt. I shall come this evening. I want to see Horst and I want to talk to his doctor and his nurse. Make sure I'm expected and there's no difficulty.'

'All right. If that's what you want, Trina, but –'

Gunther sighed and put down the receiver. Trina had cut him off in mid-sentence. He swore softly.

'Trouble?'

Gunther swung round. Nurse Braun was standing inside the main door which cut the apartment off from the rest of the clinic. He hadn't heard her come in. Until she spoke, he had thought himself alone, except for Zabel in the bedroom next door. Mentally he re-ran the conversation he had just had with Trina. There was nothing to it, but all the same he disliked the woman listening.

'The patient will have a visitor this evening,' he said coldly. 'You had better warn the Director.'

'He's not in today.'

'What?'

'His wife phoned a short while ago to say he's unwell and won't be coming to the clinic.'

'What's wrong with him?'

'I don't know. She never said. But don't worry, *mein Herr*, I can do everything for the patient that's necessary, and answer any questions the visitor would care to put.'

Gunther smiled at Marta Braun, but without affection. Keller had vouched for her, and he had enough medical knowledge to appreciate that an experienced nurse was essential, but he had never wholly trusted the Braun woman, and now he felt his doubts grow. There was something strangely self-satisfied about her today, as if she had suddenly realized that some possibility was within her grasp.

Blackmail? If Keller was really ill they could be dependent on Nurse Braun. Was that the way her mind was working? Gunther, still smiling, crossed the room to confront her.

'Of course. We can cope – with your help,' he said. 'But what do you think? Is the old boy really ill, or has he panicked?'

Marta Braun hesitated. In a sense, she was being asked to choose sides, and it was not an easy choice. She had little respect for the law, but she had never before been faced with men like the patient and Gunther. Even in her own mind she avoided the word 'terrorists'. But it was clear to her that Claude Keller had become something of a broken reed, and she had to think of herself; after all, it was Claude's fault that she was so committed.

'I'd guess he's a bit scared,' she said, 'in case the operation's turned out badly.'

Arndt Gunther became perfectly still. 'Is that at all likely?' His voice was level and frighteningly expressionless.

'No. No, of course it's not.' Marta Braun was flustered by Gunther's reaction. 'Claude – Herr Doktor Keller has one of the finest reputations, but –'

'But what?' Gunther prompted.

'Never before has he operated on such an – an important person. Perhaps it's to be expected he should be a little worried.'

Marta Braun had chosen her words carefully. She was rewarded by a satisfied nod of Gunther's head. Relieved, she went into the bedroom to attend to her patient, shutting the door behind her. Gunther, scarcely waiting for her to be gone, tapped out the Kellers' private number.

Madame Keller answered the phone herself. It was quite impossible to speak to the doctor, she told Gunther. He was unwell, and that was that. However, she did agree, albeit reluctantly, to take a message to him. She went upstairs to his bedroom at once.

Claude Keller was lying in bed, unwashed and unshaven. He was staring straight up at the ceiling. He had drunk a cup of coffee, but otherwise had left untouched the breakfast the maid had brought up to him. He showed no interest in his wife's arrival until she mentioned Gunther's name.

'I have a telephone message for you, Claude. A Herr Gunther wished to speak to you. He was very insistent, but I said you were ill and taking no calls.'

'You shouldn't have done that!' Keller turned his head and glared at her.

'Those were your instructions earlier this morning,' she replied coldly. 'Anyway, he left a message, as I said. What on earth's the matter with you, Claude? You look ghastly, and –'

'What message?' Keller quickly interrupted her.

'He said that your patient would be receiving a visit at the clinic this evening from a close friend who would wish to discuss the case with you.' Madame Keller sniffed. 'He implied that they expected you to be there, whether you're ill or not.'

'A close friend? Did he give a name? Did you ask?'

Madame Keller gave her husband yet another curious glance. 'Yes, Herr Gunther volunteered it.'

She repeated the name, and Claude Keller groaned aloud and turned his face into the pillow. It was the name of a Nazi General on whom he had operated all those years ago.

★

Trina Hansen arrived at the Clinique de la Rocque promptly at eight o'clock that evening. As far as she could tell, no one appeared to pay any attention to her at the Director's private entrance. Gunther was waiting for her, with Nurse Braun. Once safely in the sitting-room he waved her towards a half-open door.

'He's expecting you, and Nurse Braun here is just going to get Dr Keller.'

'Thanks.'

Trina felt unusually diffident as she went into the bedroom. To her surprise Horst Zabel was up and dressed, sitting in an armchair. He held out his arms and she went to kneel beside him. He rumpled her hair.

'Well, *liebling*, how are you? Things not so bad? Soon they'll be even better.' Zabel's face was still heavily bandaged, but he was able to speak though with a certain amount of difficulty, and he found prolonged conversation tiring. His English had a slight American accent. 'I can't tell you how much I'm yearning to get these goddam bandages off. I want to see what the hell I look like now that damned doctor's done his worst,' he said. 'And if I look anything like that passport photograph,' he added.

'Not many more days,' Trina said consolingly.

'I'll be glad to be out of this place, too. I don't like it, Trina. The damned doctor's a bundle of nerves. You can smell the fear coming off him. And I don't trust that nurse. Maybe it's because I'm incapacitated, but . . .' He shrugged.

'This was the best we could do, Horst. Keller's said to be one of the leading European plastic surgeons. It was pure luck we had that angle on him.'

'I know, *liebling*. I'm not criticizing.' Zabel shifted his thin body in his chair. 'Tell me the next move.'

While Trina discussed her plans with Zabel, Arndt Gunther waited restlessly in the adjoining sitting-room. He was nervous. He disliked Trina being here at the clinic when there was no need; he had seen the way Marta Braun looked at her, with grudging admiration and envy – and fear. Fear enough to make her act stupidly, perhaps?

Reminded of the nurse, he wondered where she had got to. He had sent her to fetch Keller, who had arrived a couple of hours ago and said he was going to his office. Gunther hadn't objected; he guessed the man wanted a drink; certainly his appearance suggested that he could do with one. But he had been gone a long time, too long. And where was the damned nurse?

Gunther relaxed as he heard the door open. Marta Braun came in, and Gunther stiffened as he turned to her. The woman was white-faced, her eyes wide and staring, and she was alone. She tried to speak, but her voice was a mere croak. Gunther moved quickly to seize her by the shoulders and shake her.

'What is it? What's happened?'

'Claude,' she whispered. 'Claude Keller – he's – he's dead. He's shot himself. He must have put the gun in his mouth. His brains are spattered all over his desk.'

Thirteen

It was Horst Zabel who took charge. He grasped the implications of the new situation more quickly than either Trina or Gunther, and reacted almost at once. Danger always stimulated him. His fatigue dropped from him, and he set out to establish the facts by cross-questioning the woman Braun.

'You locked the door of Keller's office when you left?'

'Yes,' she paused as she watched his cold, unfriendly eyes. 'Sir,' she added.

'Will anyone be surprised to find it locked?'

'No. It's the usual practice when his secretary's gone in the evening.'

'So, who has a key?'

'Well, I have and . . .'

Marta Braun forced herself to be calm and tried to think. The questions hissing from her patient's bandaged face terrified her. 'The Supervisor would have one – she has to let the cleaners in – and I do, of course, and then there's a complete set of emergency keys at the main desk, and –'

Zabel cut her short. 'Who's likely to go in there?'

'N – no one, sir,' she stammered. 'Not tonight. The cleaners don't come on till six in the morning. He – he's sure to be found then.'

'Six o'clock!' Zabel turned to Trina and Gunther. 'We clean up. We move out. We've got plenty of time before the pigs arrive to poke their snouts into what's been happening here. Okay?'

Trina and Gunther nodded in unison; they rarely argued with Zabel. There were obvious problems – where to take

Zabel in his present condition, for instance? But there was a possible answer to that, which occurred to them all simultaneously.

Trina thought of something else. 'How long before the stitches are removed?' she asked Marta Braun suddenly.

'Sunday, Saturday at the earliest. Keller intended to take most of them out on Saturday, I think,' the nurse said quickly, eager to help. 'But it's not difficult. Tricky around the eyes, perhaps. I could do it.'

'Kind of you, but you won't be with us,' Zabel said flatly, glancing thoughtfully at Gunther. 'What you do first, Nurse Braun, is take Mr Gunther along to the office. We must make sure the poor doctor didn't leave any incriminating papers behind. Where are my case notes?'

'Here, in this drawer,' Marta Braun said, pointing to a dressing table at one side of the bedroom. 'But you're quite right – there may be something in the office,' she agreed. She had no wish to see the body again, but she couldn't refuse. She gave Gunther what pretended to be a smile.

'Right,' Zabel said in his harsh whisper. 'Get on with it then, while we make arrangements to go and stay with our helpful friend in Geneva.'

As Marta Braun turned towards the door Gunther looked sharply at Zabel, who raised his hand and made an unmistakable gesture. Gunther, who had been expecting it, acknowledged the command with the briefest of nods. Nurse Braun noticed nothing. She went with Gunther, if not gladly, at least willingly.

'I'll phone Maidment,' Trina said when the door of the apartment had closed behind them. 'Let's hope he's there.'

Zabel didn't speak. He had given his orders, and for the moment he could rest. He still felt weak – mostly as a result of the bullet the French security man had put in him – and this infuriated him, but it was something he had to endure. Trina and Arndt could take care of the details, he thought.

*

Rory Maidment had started the day with an inadequate breakfast and drunk his lunch. The innumerable cups of coffee with which Jean Rodway had presented him during the afternoon had had little effect. And since reaching home that evening he had consumed a considerable amount of hard liquor.

He wasn't drunk, but he was feeling the impact of the whisky and, in an effort to avoid the worst of what he suspected would be a monumental hangover, was heating up some soup. This, with a little left-over ham and a tired salad, would have to do. Madame Bichaud had made him a meat pie, but this was the last thing he could face in his present state. If you drank enough, he thought stupidly, you didn't need to eat. He went to the sink and clumsily began to give his glass, stained brown with whisky, a proper wash instead of its usual brief rinse.

His hand slipped as he held the glass up to the light to admire the result of his labour. The glass fell, hit the tap and shattered in the sink. It wasn't until he had collected the pieces into an old newspaper that Maidment realized that a sliver had embedded itself in his finger. When he pulled it out the finger bled copiously. It was the last straw; Maidment could have wept.

He'd had a bitch of a day, so it seemed to him, with pressures building up from all sides. First, Peter Bingham had phoned from Berne to ask if he'd had any news of Derek. When he said no, Bingham had offered no comfort, but remarked pointedly that it was nearly the end of the week – something that Maidment himself was desperately trying to forget.

Then Denis Grandin had telephoned to say that Marie-Louise was improving, though slowly, which was the best one could expect. But the real reason for Grandin's call had been ominous – to give a warning that inadvertently he might have caused trouble for Maidment.

'My mind was on Marie-Louise,' Grandin had explained

apologetically. 'To be honest I couldn't recall who Geoffrey Linton was until after he asked to speak to Derek and I'd said Derek wasn't staying with us. Then I remembered.'

Maidment had groaned to himself, angry both at Grandin's error and at what he regarded as Linton's impudent persistence, and had spent the rest of the day waiting for Geoffrey's accusing voice in his ear. When no call came, he was puzzled. He found it hard to believe that a determined Geoffrey would give up so easily, and wondered how much longer he could hold him off, and what other steps – dangerous, even fatal, steps – his brother-in-law might be contemplating.

Finally, just as he was about to leave the office, Hugh Cantley had appeared. The Consul-General was vaguely apologetic. He hadn't intended to return to the UK for the weekend, but some family matter had come up, and there was a chap he wanted to see at the FCO. He appreciated that technically Rory was still on leave, but if he didn't mind taking over . . .

It was impossible for him to say so, but Maidment minded like hell. Cantley planned to leave early the next morning, Friday, and return on Monday, which meant that for the best part of four days – days that Rory Maidment feared – he would be in charge of the Consulate. True, it was largely the weekend, and there would be a duty clerk, but in a post like Geneva consular services were constantly in demand, and he was almost certain to be consulted. Any other time he wouldn't have cared. Now the responsibility was an extra burden he could have done without.

His finger was still bleeding, though he was holding it under the cold water tap. And he had got blood on his shirt. It was amazing how such a small cut could bleed so freely. Maidment sighed heavily.

As he did so he suddenly became aware that the phone was ringing. Unable to find a handkerchief he seized a tea-towel and wound it round his hand. He ran, stumbling in his haste.

'Hello. Maidment here.'

'Ah! You've taken your time answering. I thought you were out.'

Anger cloaked the relief in Trina Hansen's voice, but Maidment noticed neither. He was merely grateful to hear from her. The worst of all possibilities would have been a total blank – silence, until he was forced to accept that Derek's disappearance could no longer be concealed.

'No. I've been waiting. You said you'd let Derek –'

'Listen to me!' Trina cut in. 'Are you alone?'

'What do you mean – alone? Of course I'm –'

'Is there anyone in the house with you?' Trina interrupted again. 'Are you expecting anyone tonight or tomorrow?'

'No.'

'Okay. Then we're coming to see you.'

'To see me? Here? You mean, you're bringing Derek?' For a moment hope suffused Maidment, and he felt a flood of gratitude towards this unknown woman who was going to return his son to him, safe and well. Then . . .

'What in God's name do you mean – with Derek?' Momentarily Trina, in her turn, lost her grip on the conversation. Then she recovered herself. 'No, of course not. At least, not yet. But there, yes, there – at your house. Make sure your car's in the courtyard. We shall want to drive straight into the garage.'

Maidment had returned to reality. 'When do I get Derek back?' he demanded.

'Soon. A day or two later than expected.' Trina controlled her irritation. 'We've had to change our plans slightly. We'll be with you in an hour or so. Be ready, Mr Maidment.'

The line went dead, but it was several seconds before Maidment replaced his receiver. He gritted his teeth and swore silently. His not to reason why, he thought. His to do as he was told. He had better 'be ready'. Ready to help them with further plans? Had something gone badly awry? He found himself hoping, praying, that it hadn't, aware that he was totally on their side, because otherwise . . .

'That's okay,' Trina said, returning to Zabel. 'We'll deal with Maidment when we get there and have had a look at his house.'

She began to tidy away the signs of Zabel's occupancy of the bedroom and bathroom. There were few, for they had largely relied on Keller and the clinic to provide what was necessary. Moving out without leaving obvious traces would be simple and quick.

She was checking the sitting-room when Gunther returned. He gave her a brief nod of reassurance and together they went through to Zabel, who lifted his bandaged face inquiringly.

'Satisfactory. Keller's dead. He'd put a Walther P38 in his mouth, as she said. Messy, but no chance of a mistake.' Gunther spoke quite dispassionately. 'He was a businesslike guy. He left a note saying no one was to blame, and he'd done it because he couldn't bear to go on living. It was ideal – nice and vague, with no reasons – so I left it where it was.'

'And the woman?' Zabel asked.

'No problem. I borrowed Keller's gun. I don't think Braun suspected anything till the last minute. I arranged matters a bit, and with any luck it'll look like an *affaire de cœur*. I expect she and Keller took care, but some people in the clinic must have known she was his mistress.'

'I doubt if it'll deceive the pigs for long, but that doesn't matter,' Zabel said. 'Did anyone see you?'

'Entering or leaving the office? No. That wing of the place seemed deserted.'

'Good,' Trina said. 'We're about ready to go then. We can discuss how best to cope with Maidment on the way.'

She tossed Gunther the keys of the BMW and, taking their one small bag, he went to fetch the car, bringing it up close to the private entrance to the apartment. At least Zabel could walk now; on his arrival at the clinic Gunther had had to carry him. There was no trouble and they drove away without attracting any attention.

Zabel sat well back in a corner of the rear of the car, an old fishing hat of Keller's that Trina had found in a cupboard pulled well down to hide his bandages. Gunther sat beside him and Trina drove. They were all tense. The situation was not to their liking. It only needed some kind of spot check on vehicles, some mishap to the car, and a face at the window would make a polite request for identification papers.

In the event they reached the Rue de Haut without incident, and drove slowly past the entrance to the courtyard where Maidment lived. There were no signs of untoward activity and they could see that Maidment's Jaguar was in the courtyard and that the garage doors were open. But they took no chances. Trina turned at the end of the street and drove slowly back, stopping just short of the archway to let Gunther out.

'Give me ten minutes,' he said. 'If I'm not back by then, get moving. If there's a trap, I shan't know where you've gone, so I can't tell them. But it looks all right.'

With a casual wave as if he'd been dropped off after a party, Gunther left them. Five minutes later Trina restarted her engine; Zabel grunted, but said nothing. After eight minutes the tension in the BMW was palpable. Then Gunther reappeared, waving them into the courtyard and the garage.

As the car stopped Trina expelled an audible breath and Horst Zabel let his eyes close for a moment. Gunther had followed them into the garage, pulling the door down behind him. He was grinning triumphantly.

'The house could scarcely be better,' he said. 'Large bedroom with bathroom and dressing-room *en suite*. I've got Maidment putting clean sheets on right now. He's moving to a room at the far end where there's another bathroom. Cleaning woman doesn't come again till next Tuesday.'

'And Maidment? Any trouble? What did you tell him?'

'None at all. I just said that Mrs Carpenter and I needed a

131

safe house for a few days. He knew what I meant, all right. I didn't mention Horst. No reason for him to know that Horst's in the place, except perhaps for food, and I know we can fix that.'

'Then make sure he's out of the way and get me inside.' Zabel was tired and impatient. 'No need for Trina to come. She can push off back to the hotel till tomorrow. Okay?'

Trina was a little reluctant. She would have preferred to remain with Zabel, but she had to return to the hotel at some point to collect her luggage and pay her bill, and there was no reason to raise even the shadow of suspicion by a sudden, late-night departure. Better to check out in the morning, saying her boyfriend wasn't able to rejoin her as she'd hoped, and so she was leaving Geneva. Make it casual.

'Okay, Horst,' she said. She helped him from the car and, watched by a sardonic Gunther, kissed his hands. 'Till tomorrow.'

★

Maidment sat on the end of his unmade bed in one of the spare rooms, watching out of the window and listening. He saw the BMW leave, though he couldn't make out who was driving it, and reflected bitterly that this was the car that had been responsible for Marie-Louise's 'accident' – something else he owed this bloody mob.

Suddenly there was a loud squeak from the front of the house, and his head came up. He knew that sound; it was the top step but one of the main staircase, and it always squeaked, though usually not so loudly. Then he heard the mutter of voices, two voices, instantly hushed. Mr or Mrs Carpenter – whichever of them hadn't driven off in the BMW – and someone else, someone they'd not wanted him to see. It wasn't difficult to put a name to his uninvited guest; he'd bet a hundred to one it was the man he had brought into Switzerland, the wanted terrorist whom Peter Bingham thought was called Horst Zabel.

Fourteen

Arndt Gunther slept lightly, constantly coming awake as the old house gave a particularly loud creak, or Zabel snored. Other than to kick off his shoes he hadn't undressed and he had ignored the bed in the dressing-room. Instead, pulling up a couple of chairs, he had done his best to make himself comfortable inside the door leading from the bedroom to the corridor. He didn't believe Maidment would try any tricks, but he preferred to be prepared.

When grey light finally crept around the edges of the curtains and filled the room, Gunther abandoned his attempts to sleep. He lay on his back, listening to Zabel's rhythmic breathing, and thought about Trina. It was just on seven when he smelt coffee. Getting up from his improvised couch, he stretched to relieve his cramped muscles, and went downstairs.

'Good morning, Mr Maidment.'

'What's good about it?' said Maidment.

Gunther remained at his most courteous. 'Shall we say it brings nearer the day when we shall all be gone, when you'll be reunited with your son, and this unpleasant episode in your life can be forgotten?'

Maidment, as yet unwashed and unshaved, was sitting at the kitchen table in a towelling robe. A pot of coffee was in front of him, and he was buttering toast. He had slept heavily and restlessly, thanks to the amount of liquor he had drunk, but he felt the reverse of refreshed. He was still tired, bad-tempered, and in no mood for polite exchanges.

'If you want breakfast you can make your own,' he said

aggressively.

Gunther grinned. 'That's no way to treat a house-guest, Mr Maidment, but I'll settle for coffee and toast, as usual.' He found himself a mug, helped himself to coffee and put two new pieces of bread in the toaster. He sat down opposite Maidment. 'You're up early,' he added.

'The office opens at eight-thirty and I have to be in before then. My boss is going to London today, and I'll be in charge of the Consulate.'

Maidment checked himself. Why should he volunteer irrelevant information? But Gunther seemed interested, and nodded. 'Okay. You wouldn't be thinking of doing anything clever like reporting unwanted guests, would you?'

Maidment shook his head resignedly. The situation hadn't changed because the terrorists were under his roof, except perhaps for the worse. In a sense, he was now more isolated than ever. He daren't tell Peter Bingham what had happened; in the new circumstances, Bingham's reply was certain – he would demand immediate action.

'It would be tough on young Derek, very tough, if you did.'

'You don't have to remind me.'

'No? That's good.' Gunther pushed away the English marmalade. 'Haven't you got any *confiture* – any jam?'

Maidment, his mouth set, paused a moment before pushing back his chair and going to a cupboard. 'Strawberry or cherry, sir? Or would you prefer honey?'

'Strawberry'll be fine.' Gunther ignored the sarcasm.

Maidment returned to the table and poured himself a second mug of coffee. He needed it. His head still ached and his stomach was queasy. It was absurd, he thought, to be having breakfast – and making conversation – with this man whom he hated and feared, but there seemed no alternative.

From upstairs came the sound of a lavatory being flushed and Gunther said, 'Mrs Carpenter must be awake. I'd better take her up some breakfast.'

Maidment sipped his coffee. He was fairly certain that it was not Mrs Carpenter who was upstairs, but he had no intention of giving away his suspicion about the second 'house-guest'. Over the rim of his mug he studied the man opposite him and said casually, 'If you want a tray, there's one over there. What does she have for breakfast?'

There was a noticeable pause before Gunther replied, 'Oh, just toast and coffee, like me.' In fact, he was remembering what Zabel had been able to eat at the clinic. Presumably he should continue with the same sort of diet for the few days till his bandages came off. Then he must regain his strength. 'A boiled egg, maybe,' he added.

'Help yourself. I'm sure you will anyway.' Maidment gestured towards the refrigerator and stood up. 'I'm going to dress.'

'Keep to your own quarters,' Gunther said sharply.

'Of course.' Maidment turned in the doorway. 'Look. Couldn't you tell me? When can I expect this – this business to be over? There are practical problems, you know – and they affect you as much as me. Derek will be due back at school soon, for instance. I'll have to make excuses, or there'll be questions asked.'

'Sure. We understand.' Gunther pretended to think. Everything depended on keeping Maidment cooperative; the balance between threat and promise was all-important. 'Let's see. I'd guess Wednesday or Thursday. But I tell you what: we should know on Sunday and, if Mrs Carpenter agrees, we'll arrange for you to speak to your boy and we'll make a firm date for Nana Smith to drop him off somewhere he recognizes, so he can easily find his way to his aunt and uncle. How's that?'

'That's great. Thanks.'

Maidment left the kitchen and went slowly up what had been the servants' staircase. Momentarily his physical and mental wretchedness – and with them his hangover – had ceased to trouble him. Mr Carpenter had given him real

135

hope. For the first time his enemies had set out their scenario – had made clear what they planned and how Derek was to be returned safely. And, Rory Maidment told himself fiercely, *nothing* else mattered.

★

As he drove to the office, Maidment's spirits remained high. Once there, with Hugh Cantley away, he was kept busy, and it was not until after lunch that he had time to deal with some of his own affairs.

He started by telephoning Derek's school and speaking to the headmaster. Derek, he said, was not well, and would be late returning for the summer term. His apologies were received with sympathy, and messages sent to Derek.

His next call was not so simple. One difficulty was to recall exactly what he had told the Lintons previously. And Julia, while no less sympathetic, was far more curious and persistent. 'A recurrent fever?' she repeated doubtfully. 'How long has he had this, Rory? What do the doctors say? He's not staying with the Grandins now, is he?'

Maidment made his lies as vague as possible, so vague in fact that his sister grew exasperated. 'For heaven's sake, Rory!' she exclaimed. 'What on earth is going on?'

'I'm trying to tell you.' Maidment resorted to part of the truth. 'Marie-Louise is in hospital. She had an accident riding a friend's motor bike. She's getting better, but it's a slow business, and Derek had to leave.'

Julia made the right noises, but refused to be side-tracked. 'So where is he now? With you? And when did this happen?'

Maidment ducked the question of timing; he found it hard to remember just when he had last spoken to Geoffrey. 'No,' he said. 'He's with some friends in Berne.'

'Peter Bingham? But who's looking after him –'

'No, not Peter. Some friends you don't know.'

'But that's ludicrous. If he can't be with you, he'd be better off with us. He doesn't have to go back to school. And if he can be moved to Berne, you can bring him to London, or Geoffrey –'

'No, I can't!' Maidment had had enough. 'Julia, I'm at the office. Cantley's away and I'm up to my eyes in work. I've got to go now. Goodbye, and love to you and Geoffrey. And I'm so glad you're feeling well again.'

He hung up on Julia's doubtful, 'But –'. Two down and one to go, he thought, and he'd left the most difficult till last. With any luck Julia and Geoffrey could be fobbed off for a while longer, but Bingham was a different matter. Perhaps it had been a mistake to seek his help in the first place, because once Peter knew the facts he was involved, and his involvement, however vicarious, necessarily meant officialdom. It was vital to find some way of persuading Bingham to delay action for a few more days.

While he was pondering his tactics, Jean Rodway appeared. Eyes bright, cheeks flushed, she looked excited. She hadn't stopped to take off her raincoat before coming through to his office. 'Mr Maidment!'

'Yes, what is it?'

She ignored his obvious impatience. 'The Clinique de la Rocque, Mr Maidment. Are you still interested in it?'

Maidment temporized. 'Why?'

'Because – because the Director's killed himself, and a nurse has been shot dead.' The words tumbled from her as, pleased with the sudden attentiveness of her audience, she retailed the story she had heard over lunch from her friend married to the Swiss doctor. 'It'll all be on the news tonight, I expect. And it's an awful pity, apparently. Dr Keller's said to be one of the finest plastic surgeons in Europe.'

'A plastic surgeon.'

Jean frowned, taking the remark as a question. 'Yes, Mr Maidment. You knew that. It was in the file I gave you.'

'Yes, of course,' Maidment said absently. In fact, he had been talking to himself. When he read the file the specialist qualifications of the Director of the clinic had seemed no more or less relevant than those of any of the other doctors. Now he realized how wrong he might have been. 'You said the Director killed himself? What about the nurse?'

'No one really knows yet what happened. They were only found early this morning and the police are still making inquiries. But the rumour is that he shot her, then himself. She was his mistress. They say it was common knowledge at the clinic that they often spent the night together in his private apartment there.'

'He had a private apartment? At the clinic?'

Jean looked at Maidment reproachfully. 'You didn't really read that file, did you, Mr Maidment?'

'Yes, I did, Jean, but I was tired, and I'm afraid I didn't take in all of it.' Maidment tried to grin apologetically. 'But thanks a lot. Let me know if you hear any more.'

Maidment turned to the papers on his desk, but his thoughts were elsewhere. As far as he knew, the police had got nowhere with the murder of Monsieur Le Gros; according to the media there had been few leads. But the death of the Director of the Clinique de la Rocque and his nurse and mistress would be a different matter, and the investigation would be pursued more assiduously. Certainly the event would attract wide publicity, at least in Switzerland. And Peter Bingham, knowing what he did, would have to be very stupid not to see instantly the obvious connection between it and the terrorist he believed to be Horst Zabel.

Towards the end of the afternoon Maidment reluctantly phoned the Embassy in Berne, but only to be told that Bingham had left for the weekend. Having explained who he was and that the call was urgent, he was put on to a colleague of Bingham's whom he knew. The colleague sounded flippant, but was eager to be helpful.

'You could try the Embassy in Bonn. Peter's gone to Germany. No, not a bird – on duty. But you know Peter. One can never pin him down about these trips of his. He'll be back on Tuesday, if that's any use to you.'

'It is. Many thanks.'

'Sorry not to be more help.'

But you have been, Maidment thought as he cut the connection. With Peter busy with his own affairs and unreachable till Tuesday, he had one less problem to worry about. By Sunday he might have some real news of Derek and by Tuesday, please God, be on his way to collect the boy . . .

★

Derek had been locked in his bedroom all the afternoon. Nana Smith had to go to town. There was shopping to be done, fresh food to be bought, a prescription to be filled at the chemist. She explained all this to him because she expected to be some time and, since he looked so woebegone at the thought of being shut up on such a lovely Spring day, she allowed him to take her transistor radio upstairs with him for company. Nevertheless, Derek's afternoon passed very slowly. NO PLUG?

For Nana Smith time went too fast. The nearby town was crowded and stuffy. She had difficulty in finding a place to park. There were queues in the shops, and she had to go to two or three pharmacists before she could find her pills. When she reached home she was tired and exhausted. It was an effort to unpack the car, and what she wanted most was to put her feet up and rest.

But there was the boy to be released and tea to be made. Slowly she plodded up to the attic. Derek wasn't listening to the radio; he had grown bored with it. He was lying on his bed, hands behind his head, staring at the ceiling. He sat up as the old woman came into the room, his face bright.

'Nana! I'm glad you're back.'

'Come down and help me get tea.' She knew that his happiness at her return was mainly because he hated to be left

139

alone in the house, but nevertheless she was pleased by it. 'I've bought you a present.'

'What? Sweeties?' He was being well fed and it wasn't that he was hungry, but to suck a sweet was consoling, as he had discovered during his first homesick days away at school. 'What sort?'

'Wait and see.'

There was a bag of toffees on the kitchen table and a paperback of John Buchan's *Greenmantle*. Derek hugged Nana Smith. 'Thank you. Thank you,' he said. Though he couldn't have explained why, somehow he felt more grateful for any small kindness that Nana Smith showed him than for all the love and care he had been accustomed to receive at home in the past.

Companionably they sat down to tea together. Derek ate buttered scones with jam, and a big slice of fruit cake. Nana Smith ate nothing, but she drank several cups of black tea. She still felt extremely tired and unsteady, and when she stood up to refill the teapot she had a sudden sharp pain that seemed to spread throughout her whole body. She had to cling to the edge of the table to prevent herself falling.

Derek looked up anxiously from his cake. 'Are you all right, Nana?'

It was a couple of seconds before she could reply. 'Yes! Don't bother me! Get on with your tea, boy!'

It was the way she spoke rather than her words that frightened Derek. Nana Smith often barked at him for no apparent reason, and he had learnt not to mind. But this was different. It wasn't as if he had done anything to irritate her. She had not only sounded angry, but also as if she were not here, standing right beside him, but a million miles away. He watched her surreptitiously as the attack passed away and she set about making a fresh pot of tea.

To avoid another rebuke, however, he took care to concentrate on his last crumbs of cake as Nana Smith returned to her seat. Out of the corner of his eye he saw her begin to put down the teapot and he cried out a warning. Too late. Somehow she had misjudged her distances. For a moment the pot balanced on the edge of the table; then it fell with a crash to the floor. Simultaneously Nana Smith pitched sideways out of her chair to lie amid bits of broken china, tea and tealeaves.

Derek's natural instinct was to help, but Nana Smith was a big woman and he couldn't possibly move her. Almost automatically he picked up the broken china around her, did his best to mop up the tea, straightened her skirt and fetched a cushion to put under her head. She was breathing heavily, so he knew she wasn't dead, but she showed no sign of waking.

It was only then that it occurred to Derek that he could escape. The front door key would be in Nana's bag, there on the dresser, and there was nothing to prevent him from unlocking it, unfastening any bolts and chains it might have, and running down the road. He had no idea of his whereabouts, except that he was still in England, but sooner or later he would meet someone or come to a bus stop or . . . He had no money, but again his eye lighted on Nana's bag. Surely he could get himself back to Aunt Julia and Uncle Geoffrey.

Then he thought that if he ran away Nana might lie on the floor until she died, all by herself. He couldn't possibly just leave her. He must do something to help. As his initial shock passed, he tried to remember what you did for people who fainted or had accidents. Keep them warm. Put blankets round them. Brandy. Loosen anything tight. Send for a doctor.

A doctor! The telephone! Of course! There it was, high up on a shelf, but he could easily reach it from a chair. And if he could phone for a doctor, why not his aunt or uncle – or even his father?

But would they be pleased to hear from him? Or to see him if he ran away? Derek shook his head doubtfully. His father had said he must stay with Nana Smith for a few days – days that had stretched and stretched until there seemed no end to them. But did his father know he was locked up each night and sometimes during the day? Did he know he wasn't allowed beyond the garden? Did he know how miserable and lonely he was? And, he wondered, did he really care? His father had wished him a happy birthday, but there had been no presents – except from Nana.

His dilemma was solved for him as Nana Smith stirred slightly. Quickly he undid the tight buttons at the throat of her blouse, fetched the duvet from his bed and, after a short search, found a half-bottle of brandy in a kitchen cupboard. As he lifted her head, and tried to persuade her to swallow some, Nana Smith spoke.

'Pills,' she murmured. 'In bag.'

Derek got the pills, gave her water and, after a while, helped her to sit up. It wasn't until the next day that she asked him why he hadn't run away. He said, 'I thought of it. I nearly did, but I couldn't leave you like that, ill and alone, could I?'

Nana Smith didn't answer.

Fifteen

Julia Linton, wearing only a bra and slip, was sitting at her dressing-table and frowning at her reflection in the glass. She hadn't felt up to going to the hairdressers, but Mrs Walker, who at present came in every weekday, had helped to wash and set her hair, and had done a more than adequate job. It was looking its best, but it framed a face that was pale under the make-up. The brown eyes were anxious and there were lines etched in the skin that hadn't been there before the accident. Quickly Julia transformed her features into a smile as Geoffrey came into the room.

'Admiring yourself, darling? If you are, you've got every justification.' He bent and kissed his wife's bare shoulder. 'You look lovely – but a mite tired. Are you sure you want to go to this dinner party?'

'Of course. Besides, we can't cry off at the last moment. It would be most unfair to the Grants.'

'Okay, if you're certain.'

'Positive.' Julia slipped some amethyst earrings through her lobes, and did up the clasp of a matching necklace. She pushed back the dressing-table stool, and stood up carefully; her thigh from which the piece of metal had been extracted still bothered her. With equal care she stepped into the yellow silk dress that had been lying over the back of a chair. 'Zip me up, Geoffrey,' she said.

Linton, who had been watching his wife's careful movements, did as he was asked, silently cursing the two men who were the cause of her distress. Nothing more had been learnt about them, and there had been no attempt at blackmail.

Either the accident had been just that – an accident – or the intention to put pressure on him had been abandoned. Inquiries seemed to have come to a dead-end, the matter neatly filed.

'We can come home early, you know – whenever you want to,' he said. 'The Grants will understand. It's only a small affair, six or eight people, and quite informal.'

In fact, that evening they were to be a party of nine in the tall Highgate house where the Grants lived. Jack Grant apologized for the squash it would create around the dining-table, but he explained that, lunching at his club, he'd met an old friend whom he'd not seen for ages and who was only in London for the weekend. He beamed on his other guests. Grant was a jovial character, red-faced and overweight, who looked more like an archetypal farmer or publican than the successful barrister that he was.

'I hope he's not going to be late,' Simone Grant said, consulting her watch.

Simone, a dark, thin, woman, elegant in a tight black dress, was a French Canadian. She was an expert cook, and prided herself on her little dinner parties. Informal they might be, but the food was important, and she expected her guests to be punctual. If this man who was upsetting her table didn't appear in the next five minutes . . . But the doorbell rang almost immediately, and Simone was mollified by profuse apologies and a dozen white roses.

'Come along in and meet everyone,' she said as they greeted the new arrival in the hall. 'Jack, you do the introductions.'

Grant introduced the three couples who were standing in a semi-circle. 'And this is my old chum, Hugh Cantley. Believe it or not, we were at school together. Whisky, Hugh? Gin and something?'

'Whisky and soda, please. No ice.'

Grant went to get Cantley's drink, and Geoffrey Linton remarked, 'Jack did say your name was Hugh Cantley, didn't he? Are you in the Foreign Office – Consul-General in Geneva, by any chance?'

'Yes, that's right.' Cantley raised an interrogative eyebrow.

'Then you know Rory Maidment?'

'Yes, of course. He's my deputy. But I can't say I know him well, because I've only been in Geneva a few months. Is he a friend of yours?'

'He's my brother,' Julia said.

'I see,' said Cantley, looking at Julia with interest.

Grant returned with Cantley's drink, and there was an exchange of platitudes about the smallness of the world, with examples from everyone. Then Simone came to announce that dinner was ready and they filed into the long, narrow dining-room. Julia found herself seated on her host's left, with Hugh Cantley on her other side and Geoffrey nearly opposite.

The dinner – from the lemons stuffed with salmon mousse, through the veal escalope, to the strawberries coated with Kirsch – was excellent. Conversation ranged from the latest plays in the West End to books and travel, and Grant produced some wicked anecdotes about clients and colleagues at the Bar. It was a pleasant and civilized meal and Julia enjoyed it. Geoffrey was thankful to see her looking so much like her normal self.

Coffee and liqueurs were served at the table; Simone held strong views about men staying behind to tell dirty stories over port, as she put it. And it was during coffee that Cantley, who had been the quietest member of the gathering, said, 'By the way, how's your young nephew, Mrs Linton?'

'Derek?' Julia was startled. 'Have you met him?'

'Why, no. I've had no chance. I didn't arrive *en poste* till the beginning of January, and anyway he didn't come to Geneva at Christmas because he was sick, I'm told. Now, poor child, there's been this disaster at Easter too.'

'What disaster?' Julia asked in a small voice.

'I'm sorry. I exaggerate. One shouldn't call mumps a disaster, I suppose, though it can be a serious illness, but it must have been disappointing for the boy to have two holidays in succession ruined. It was a blow for Rory, too, I assure you. He's been very worried –' Cantley stopped, suddenly aware that Mrs Linton had become pale and looked as if she were about to faint.

From across the table Geoffrey Linton said quickly, 'My wife's not been well, Mr Cantley. This is the first time she's been out since she was involved in a rather nasty car crash a couple of weeks ago. As you can imagine, we've been somewhat self-absorbed. To tell you the truth, we didn't know that Derek had mumps or that he wasn't in Geneva.'

'I – I'm so sorry. I just assumed you knew. I didn't mean to upset Mrs Linton.' Cantley looked anxiously from Linton to Julia. 'I regret having been the bearer of bad tidings,' he added a little pompously.

'Oh, please don't blame yourself, Mr Cantley,' Julia said over-politely. She had drained her brandy glass and colour had returned to her cheeks. She was now quite composed. 'Rory should have told us.'

'Probably didn't want to worry us, darling.' There wasn't a hint of sarcasm in Linton's voice. 'Poor little Derek. We must do something about him. Do you know where he is, Mr Cantley? He's not still at his school, I suppose?'

'I'm afraid I've no idea.' Cantley shook his head in regret. Then, having picked up his coffee cup, he replaced it without drinking. 'Though, come to think of it . . . Rory was in my office last week – yes, the Monday before Easter I think it was – when a Mrs Carpenter telephoned for him. He didn't say so, but I rather gathered the call was something to do with his son.'

'Mrs Carpenter!' Julia involuntarily let her surprise show. 'You know her?'

Julia looked at her husband, who shook his head slightly. 'Er – we've met,' she replied.

Simone Grant had risen and was suggesting a return to the drawing-room. As soon as they decently could the Lintons made Julia's recent accident an excuse and said they must go. There were goodnights and thanks, and promises to meet again soon, but at last the Lintons were in their car and alone.

'Geoffrey, what's happened? I don't understand.'

'I understand one thing, my dear. Your brother's been lying through his teeth. Derek never got to Geneva. It looks as if he's still here, in the UK, with Mrs Carpenter, whoever she may be.'

'Not necessarily,' Julia said thoughtfully. 'If Rory's been lying – and I agree he has – what he told Cantley may be untrue, too, or it may not be the whole truth. Derek was perfectly healthy when he left us. I don't believe for a moment he's got mumps. And this Mrs Carpenter could have taken him – anywhere.' Suddenly, as the implication of what she was saying overcame her, she suppressed a sob. 'And it's all my fault. If I'd not had that damned accident, I'd have made sure Derek got on to his plane safely and there wouldn't have been any of this – this trouble.'

'Whatever's happened, it's not your fault.' Linton spoke automatically, but with assurance. He didn't believe that Julia was in any way to blame. On the contrary. All the doubts he'd had when he had learnt that the occupants of the van that had crashed into her car were wanted terrorists came flooding back. He couldn't imagine any connection between terrorists and Rory Maidment, but . . . He temporized. 'None of it makes any sense,' he said as he swung the car with unnecessary violence into the driveway of their house.

'It's late – Geneva time's an hour ahead of us – but shall we phone Rory?' Julia suggested tentatively.

'No. What's the use? He'll only tell us more lies.'

'But we must do something, Geoffrey. I'm worried about Derek – and Rory. Rory adores that boy. He'd never let any harm come to him, but . . .'

'I know darling. There are too many "buts". If I'd not

147

known how devoted Rory was I might have been more insistent before. As it was, I let him put me off.' Linton sighed. 'After all, though we're often *in loco parentis*, Derek *is* Rory's son and it was embarrassing to interfere too much.'

'But surely now –'

'Oh yes! Now, to hell with interfering.' Linton opened the car door for Julia and helped her out. 'Time you were in bed. Time we were both in bed. Tomorrow I go to Geneva and knock the truth out of Rory.' *Fool!*

★

Geoffrey Linton arrived at Heathrow the next morning, Sunday, early – an hour before the first flight to Geneva. He hoped to return to London the same evening, but he had with him a briefcase containing a clean shirt and some toilet articles, in case he was forced to spend a night away. He checked in, then went through the controls to the airside British Airways Executive Club Lounge.

When, in spite of police requests, Mrs Carpenter had failed to come forward as a witness to the traffic accident, it was thought she might have gone on holiday abroad, and fruitless inquiries were made at airports and seaports. No inquiries, however, were made about Derek Maidment, a minor travelling alone. There had been no need; his father had confirmed that the boy had arrived safely at his destination.

This was an oversight that Linton now intended to rectify. He showed his boarding pass and his Executive Club card, and gave the girl behind the reception desk in the lounge a cheerful smile.

'I wonder if you could help me?'

'If I can, sir.' She would have given the same answer to any Club member at any time, but it was Sunday morning, she wasn't busy and Linton looked rather like her father. 'What's the difficulty?'

148

'No difficulty really, no kind of complaint, but I'd like some information. The trouble is it's a rather embarrassing family matter. You see . . .'

Linton had taken care to devise in advance what he hoped would sound a plausible story. The girl listened attentively and with sympathy.

'You mean your nephew's what the papers call a "tug-of-war" child. Is that it, sir?'

'Yes.' Geoffrey beamed at her. 'Yes, that's it, exactly. He's turned up quite safely with his father, but his mother would like to know if the friend who was supposed to put him on that Swissair flight to Geneva actually did so or not – whether she's to be trusted, in fact. I wondered if you knew anyone in Swissair who might help – off the record, as it were.'

'I understand. If you'd like to get yourself a cup of coffee, sir, I'll see what I can do.'

'Thank you very much. I'm most grateful.'

Linton collected coffee and biscuits from the bar, picked up a *Sunday Times* from the stacks of available newspapers, sat himself down in a comfortable armchair and stretched his legs in front of him. The lounge was almost empty. A couple of businessmen, papers on their knees, talked quietly in a corner. An obvious husband and wife exchanged an occasional remark. One man was on the phone, another seemingly doing some accounts. No one had turned on the television set. Outside was the muffled roar of the occasional aircraft taking off or landing. From his seat Linton could hear the receptionist muttering into her phone about a 'UM' – an Unaccompanied Minor – called Maidment on SR831 the Friday before last.

Linton drank his coffee and ate his biscuits. He glanced at the headlines, leafed through the magazine and began to read the business section. His head nodded. Neither he nor Julia had slept much the previous night, and soon he was dozing.

'Sir! Wake up, sir.'

'What?' Linton roused himself. 'Surely it can't be time for

149

my flight yet.' He looked at his watch.

'Not your flight, sir. But the information you wanted.'

'Ah, yes.' Linton passed a hand over his face. 'Have you come up with anything?'

'In a negative way, yes, sir. Derek Maidment wasn't on that flight. He was paged but he never checked in. The Swissair hostess who was meant to take charge of him remembers it clearly. It's not often that a minor fails to turn up without some explanation.'

Linton thanked her very much, and returned to his newspaper until his flight was called. She had confirmed what he had expected and feared since Hugh Cantley's remarks at the Grants' dinner party. It meant that from the very beginning – from the first phone call he'd made at Julia's insistence to check on Derek's safe arrival in Geneva, Maidment had lied.

But why? Linton watched the clouds drift past the window as the aircraft gained height, briefly turbulent. He pondered the question for the umpteenth time without finding a credible answer. Eventually he tried to sleep. By the end of the day, he told himself, he would know the truth.

Sixteen

Oddly enough, Rory Maidment slept well and woke late, with a certain sense of expectancy. Then he remembered that it was Sunday, the day on which he had been half promised news of his unwanted guests' departure and of Derek's safe return. He told himself not to be hopeful but, lying in bed, he could hear sounds that suggested considerable activity in the rooms at the other end of the house. He tried to interpret them, but with little success.

The lavatory was flushed several times. Then more running water. Baths? Showers? A great deal of washing seemed to be going on. Someone went downstairs and, after an interval, returned; by the sound of the footsteps, he (or she) was carrying something heavy. On the other hand there were no smells of breakfast. Then someone else – it was a light tread, and Maidment immediately thought of Mrs Carpenter – came along to the cupboard near his room where the linen was kept, and spent some minutes there, presumably searching for something. Maidment couldn't imagine what they were doing.

He wasn't even sure how many of them there were, though he guessed at three. On his return from the office yesterday – he had gone in to keep out of the way of his guests, rather than from any great necessity on a Saturday – he had found the blue BMW once more in his garage. It had remained there. But, however many uninvited visitors he had, they had been careful; he had still seen only the one man, the so-called Mr Carpenter, whose real name would have meant nothing to him.

★

The sounds that Maidment heard were easily explicable. Arndt Gunther was about to remove Horst Zabel's bandages and take out at least some of the stitches. And he was extremely nervous. Though he wasn't responsible for Zabel's reconstructed face, it was he who had forcibly co-opted Dr Keller's services and assisted with the operation. If Keller had done a bad job, Zabel's wrath – and Trina's – would inevitably fall on him.

'Aren't you ready yet, Arndt?' Zabel was growing impatient. 'If you're not, you never will be.'

'Yes, yes, I'm ready. But I want to take care. I'm not a qualified surgeon, you know. And I'm trying to remember . . .' By his insistence on washing, sterilizing everything as far as possible, Gunther had been putting off the moment he was dreading. Now he had to act. 'Okay,' he said, 'let's get going.'

The bed and its bolster were covered with a clean, white sheet. The pillow-case was also clean and white. Another sheet was drawn up to Zabel's chest. He and Trina and Gunther all wore some of Maidment's newly-laundered white shirts that Trina had found in the airing cupboard. Zabel had protested that Gunther was making an unnecessary fuss; the surgery was finished; he wasn't about to have it again. But Gunther had silenced him by saying that possibly one of the incisions hadn't yet healed completely, and the risk of any infection must be avoided.

Slowly the bandages were unwound and the dressings removed. It was not the simplest operation. The bed was low; Gunther had to sit sideways on it and lean towards Zabel. Zabel couldn't lie back against the pillow, and Trina had to support him. They were all tense.

Then the new face was revealed. Gunther regarded it with awe, Trina with some doubt. Gently Gunther turned Zabel's head from side to side, and she watched him anxiously.

'Come on,' Zabel said. 'For Christ's sake, let me see. Has he made a mess of it? Is it anything like the photograph?'

'It's wonderful! Wonderful! He's done a terrific job.' Gunther was grinning with relief.

'But – those marks,' Trina protested.

'Just bruising. They'll disappear very soon, and if there's any slight scarring left it won't be noticeable in a day or two. A spot of make-up'll cover it in the meantime.' Gunther was jubilant.

'Let me see,' Zabel demanded again.

Gunther pushed him back against the pillow. 'Horst, please. Just wait till I've got the stitches out. It'll look even better then. I promise you, you're going to be more than satisfied with the result.'

Removing the sutures was tedious rather than difficult. There were a great many of them, and some were incredibly fine, especially around the eyes. Nor did Gunther's uncomfortable position help. He yearned for an operating table or a high hospital bed, which would have made his task less trying. But he was reasonably adept with his hands, and at last he completed the job without more than minor discomfort to the patient.

'There!' Gunther stood up and stepped back to survey Zabel. 'The healing's perfect, and I've got them all out. There'll be no need for any more dressings or another session. You're a new man, Horst.'

'Where's the best place to see? The bathroom?'

Trina helped Zabel up, but let him go into the bathroom alone. She exchanged glances with Gunther, then shook her head in disbelief. 'It's uncanny. It *is* Horst, yet it isn't.'

'You'll get used to it. And it fits the passport photo perfectly well.'

'I know, but I'm not sure I like it.'

'Let's hope Horst does.'

They waited. Horst Zabel was taking his time, which was not surprising. After all, he had lived with his old face for forty years. He had seen it in the mirror every day, washing, shaving, cleaning his teeth, doing his hair. Naturally it had changed over the period, but so gradually that he had scarcely noticed. It had continued to be *his* face, with its familiar narrow eyes, down-turned mouth, untidy nose. Zabel had never had pretensions to good looks, any more than to a fine physique. All his life he had accepted that, and the fact that he was not a big man with classic features had never bothered him. Why should it? He'd always had as many women as he wanted, and his attributes – qualifications, one might call them – were quite different: ability to plan and carry through a plan, with ruthless determination at whatever cost to others, or himself.

But now . . . Though he had some idea what to expect from the photograph they had shown Keller, the actual result was startling. He'd known his new face would be better-looking than his old one, but he hadn't expected this. Somehow, by widening the eyes, thinning the nostrils, lifting the corners of the mouth and other deft surgical procedures, he had been transformed. His face was now almost hand-some, if a trifle expressionless. But of course the body still didn't fit; intentionally or not, that damned Doktor Keller had played a joke on him, Zabel thought wryly.

Suddenly, startling Trina and Gunther in the next room, and heard dimly by Rory Maidment at the far end of the corridor, Zabel began to laugh.

*

Half an hour later, after a light breakfast, Horst Zabel lay on his bed. Trina and Gunther had pulled up chairs to the bedside, placed close together so that he had no need to turn his head constantly from side to side. The three of them were holding a conference.

'Why can't we stick to the original plan?' Gunther said. 'Leave Geneva on Wednesday or Thursday – Horst should certainly be strong enough for the journey by then, and his face will be fine – and drive to Zurich. You two fly from there, and I'll join you later.'

'Maidment?' Zabel was succinct.

'What about him? As long as we hang on to the boy, Maidment will do as he's told.'

'Can we be sure of that?' Zabel interrupted. 'I've never met this Maidment guy, but I do know that in circumstances like this every victim's got his breaking point. Look at Keller; he broke pretty soon. And Maidment?' Zabel shrugged. 'We've been leaning on him hard.'

Trina had been studying Zabel's new face; if it held any expression at all, it registered fatigue. 'Wednesday would be best. No earlier unless we must,' she said. 'As for Maidment, it's a question of timing, isn't it? We must be well away before he realizes he's heard the last of us – and his son. Perhaps we could leave him an encouraging note to say his brat will be released in forty-eight hours. That should hold him.'

'You said you intended the boy should be set free,' Gunther reminded her.

Trina glanced at Zabel. 'We gave it some thought and finally decided against it. By now he'll know too much about Nana Smith and the house. That set-up took a long time to establish and it's valuable to us. We don't want to lose it.'

Gunther shook his head. 'I still think Maidment will make a hell of a fuss once he gives up hope for the boy.'

'So what? He knows nothing about Horst. He thinks he smuggled some drug – probably heroin – into Switzerland for us. He's never seen my face. And as for you, Arndt, you pride yourself on being unremarkable; in any case, the chances of him meeting you anywhere are negligible. Once we're out of the country there'll be damn all he, or anyone else, can do.'

'Fair enough,' said Zabel. 'But we've got to get out of the country safely. Let me see that passport again. I'm far from happy about it.'

Trina produced a West German passport and Zabel studied it. Made out in the name of one Klaus Arnheim, it had been issued two years ago in Bonn. Arnheim was described as a company director, height 1.7 metres, weight 59 kilograms, eyes and hair brown, no distinguishing marks. He was said to have been born in Köln thirty-eight years ago. He was a frequent traveller; during the past year he had been to half-a-dozen European countries, as well as North America.

'It's a good passport – a genuine one, apart from a few added entry and exit stamps,' Trina said. 'A safe one, too. We were lucky to get it, and especially lucky that Keller said he could use the face as a – a model. But we thought your hair should be a bit darker, and we've got some stuff.' She looked doubtfully at Zabel.

'Okay, I understand,' said Zabel. 'I'm not worried about that; all passport photos are pretty poor. But what about the rest of the legend?'

'We've got all that, too – from the same source as the passport. Letters, papers, identity card – even credit cards, though you shouldn't try to use them, of course.'

'All right,' Zabel said at last. 'Let's get the hair done.'

'Now?'

'Yes, right now,' Zabel replied curtly.

Trina was against it. She thought Zabel had had enough for one day. But he insisted. The sooner his hair was done, the better, he said. He wanted to be ready to move out of Maidment's house at short notice, just in case it became necessary.

How the accident happened none of them was sure. Secretly Trina and Gunther both thought Zabel's tiredness was to blame. They were in the bathroom. Zabel was sitting in front of the wash basin and Trina was about to apply the colour, which she poured from its bottle into a cereal bowl that Gunther had fetched from the kitchen. Zabel reached rather clumsily for an extra towel. And the bowl was knocked into the basin, its contents gurgling thickly down the drain.

'You've got some more of this stuff?'

'No.'

'Then get some, right away.'

'Horst, it's Sunday. We can't.'

'There must be a pharmacy open, even on a Sunday. Isn't that where you buy it?' Zabel fatigue was expressing itself in growing irritation.'

To save an argument, Gunther said he would ask Maidment and go and see what could be done. In any case, he reflected, he had been almost house-bound since Zabel had reached Geneva and he felt in need of air and exercise. Maidment, whom he found in the kitchen making himself breakfast, wasn't much help, but he did suggest one of two stores that might be open.

As Gunther was about to leave Maidment said, 'Have you reached any decisions yet?'

'Decisions?' Gunther looked blank.

'When you're leaving here, when Derek –'

'We go on Wednesday. And Derek –' Remembering the conversation upstairs, Gunther hesitated. 'Twelve hours after we've gone,' he said briefly.

'Thanks.'

Three, four more days at most, Maidment thought. Whatever happened he must make sure that no one interfered before then.

★

Some ten minutes after Gunther left the house a taxi turned into the courtyard. Geoffrey Linton got out, paid the driver and rang the front door bell. He didn't look up, or he might have seen Trina Hansen at a window. Trina had heard the taxi and gone to see who it was.

'I don't know,' she said to Zabel. 'A tall man, pin-stripe suit, briefcase. He looks like some kind of official.' She

157

frowned. 'He would come when Arndt's not here.'

'Go and listen at the top of the stairs,' Zabel ordered.

Trina, still wearing Maidment's shirt, softly opened the bedroom door and went out into the corridor. She watched from the landing as Maidment came from the kitchen into the hall. The bell rang again, lengthily, almost angrily. At last Maidment opened the front door.

'Geoffrey!' Trina heard him exclaim.

'Hello, Rory.'

Linton regarded his brother-in-law coldly. He took in the unshaven face, the pyjamas, dressing gown and slippers, but especially the look of surprise and horror with which Maidment greeted him. Linton told himself that he hadn't expected to be welcomed, and he'd been right.

'May I come in?'

'Yes, of course.' With obvious reluctance Maidment took a step back so that he no longer blocked the doorway. 'I – er – was just having breakfast,' he said. 'It's Sunday,' he added lamely, as if to excuse the hour.

Linton followed him into the sitting-room. Upstairs Trina, who had heard the conversation and realized the identity of the unexpected visitor, swiftly returned to Zabel. She was pulling off Maidment's shirt, reaching for her corduroy slacks and a top. She made sure her small 9 mm Makarov pistol was in a pocket.

'Trouble,' she said. 'It's Linton, Maidment's brother-in-law from London. Come to investigate, do you think? I may have to go down.'

Dressed, she ran her fingers through her hair and, without waiting for an answer, went quietly back to the landing. Their luck, she thought bitterly, had run out. If necessary she would kill them both, but . . . She listened, but could hear no voices. Cautiously she descended a couple of stairs, wincing as they squeaked, and peered through the banisters. She could see Linton in the sitting-room, hands behind his back, gazing through the window into the courtyard. There was no sign of Maidment, until he appeared with a tray.

'Here we are, Geoffrey. Coffee. You said you'd had an early lunch on the plane. Come and sit down.'

'Thanks.' Linton didn't sound in the least grateful. 'Rory, you know why I'm here, don't you?'

'No. Should I?' Suddenly Maidment seemed anxious. 'It's not Julia, is it? A change for the worse?'

'No, no! Julia's fine.' Linton was impatient. He wished he had refused coffee; getting it had given Rory time to recover from his surprise and compose himself. 'It's Derek, of course.'

'Derek? What about him? He's fine.' Remembering what he'd told Julia, Maidment added quickly, 'This fever of his is low-grade, nothing serious, but best to keep him out of school.'

'The aftermath of his mumps, I presume?' Linton was sarcastic. 'Rory, I'm tired of your lies. I want the truth. I know Derek didn't catch the flight to Geneva he was meant to. I've checked at Heathrow. I know he wasn't staying with the Grandins when you said he was. In fact, Julia and I don't believe he ever arrived in Geneva. You told your superior, Cantley, and doubtless the rest of your office, that Derek couldn't come because he had mumps. You told Julia and me quite a different story. A succession of lies. We want to know why.'

There was a long pause. Then Maidment said quietly, 'Suppose we take your – er – accusations one by one, Geoffrey. First, Derek's arrival. You're quite right. I did lie to you about that. He wasn't on his intended flight, as you say. He missed it because he was sick on the way to the airport, not through any fault of Mrs Carpenter's. On the contrary, she was extremely kind. She took him home with her, phoned me and put him on a later flight. I didn't mention it because you and Julia obviously had enough worries at that particular moment, and I didn't want to add to them.'

'Go on!' It was a plausible story, Linton thought, but somehow he sensed that it wasn't the truth, or at least not the whole truth.

'Okay. Now, the Grandins,' Maidment said, and on the stairs Trina relaxed a little; this part would be relatively simple, she guessed. 'Denis phoned me. You'd bothered him. He didn't understand what you were getting at. Derek had been staying with them, but naturally he had to leave when Marie-Louise had her motor-cycle accident.'

'And now he's staying with friends in Berne, though he's not well.'

'Geoffrey, he's staying with his godfather, Peter Bingham. If you don't believe me, call Peter and ask him.' Maidment spoke with apparent confidence – confidence born of the knowledge that Peter Bingham was away for the weekend. 'Go on! There's the phone. Be my guest. Here's Peter's home number. Look, I'll write it down for you. For heaven's sake, what's got into you? Why this – this interrogation? What on earth do you think I've done with Derek?'

Linton hesitated. The last question was one he and Julia had asked themselves over and over again, and found no answer. He changed the subject. 'What do you know about this Mrs Carpenter?'

'What I've told you. She seems to have been kind to Derek, and I'm grateful to her.'

'When she phoned, didn't she tell you where she lived or give you a number?'

'No. She did not. If she had I'd have told you before, when you said the police wanted her as a witness to Julia's accident. It's not my fault she's not come forward.'

Linton regarded his brother-in-law doubtfully. He was beginning to wish he had never come to Geneva. Maidment seemed to have an answer for everything, and yet . . .

'Why did you tell Hugh Cantley Derek had mumps?' he asked suddenly.

'Mumps? Ah, yes. You mentioned mumps before.' Maidment slowly finished his coffee. 'It was the first thing that came into my head, to be honest. If the office had known Derek was in Geneva, they'd have expected him to be around, especially as we've been busy and I've had to work, and a lot of my colleagues – especially those with kids of their own – would have wanted to entertain him. I decided that it was best for him to be kept fairly quiet.'

It was a specious excuse, and Maidment knew it, but he could think of nothing else. Linton didn't bother to hide his incredulity as another point occurred to him.

'You're sure you know no more about this Mrs Carpenter than you've told me, Rory? According to Cantley, she telephoned you at your office on the Monday after Derek was due to arrive.' Linton stood up. 'So what did she say then?'

'Oh, for God's sake, Geoffrey!' Maidment raised his voice, and hesitated. 'Look,' he said finally, 'Derek is with Peter Bingham. As I said, if you don't believe me, phone him. I assume you'd take his word for it?'

Linton seemed to debate the question. And from upstairs came the sound of a loud sneeze which Zabel had failed to suppress. Linton stiffened. 'Who's that?'

Trina didn't wait for Maidment to attempt an answer. She reacted immediately, and ran down the stairs.

It was hard to say which of the two men was the more surprised when she appeared in the sitting-room, but she gave neither of them any time to think. 'Oh!' she said. 'I heard the doorbell, but I didn't know you had a visitor, darling.'

To Linton, she added immediately, 'I'm Catherine Carter,' and to Maidment with a smile, 'Introduce him, dear.'

Maidment hastily collected his wits. He knew that she was Mrs Carpenter, for he recognized her voice, but he found this attractive girl so different from his imaginings . . . 'Er – this is Geoffrey Linton, my brother-in-law,' he said, hoping that Geoffrey would attribute any hesitation to an embarrassment that was so clearly justified by the apparent circumstances.

Linton's reaction was to repeat the new arrival's name. 'Catherine – Carter?'

'That's right, but call me Catherine, please.'

For a second Linton had thought she'd said 'Carpenter'. But, like Maidment's, though for different reasons, his mind had balked at the idea. This girl didn't fit the description of the prim, middle-aged, grey-haired woman that the witnesses of the accident had provided. He smiled at her thinly.

'I wasn't expecting to meet you till Friday, Mr Linton,' Trina continued, returning the smile. 'Or will it be your wife who's meeting us at Heathrow?'

'I don't understand,' Linton said blankly.

'Oh, Rory can't have got around to telling you yet. I have to return to London next Friday and we thought that, if Derek's well enough, I could bring him over and deliver him to you.' She turned to Maidment. 'Can you remember the flight number offhand.'

'Er – no,' Maidment said, as they both looked at him expectantly. He searched for an adequate response. 'I think it's the usual first British Airways flight; it gets in between ten and eleven. But I'll phone and give Julia the details.' He paused. 'Will that be – satisfactory, Geoffrey?'

Linton nodded. His mouth was set. Carpenter – Carter, he was thinking. Hugh Cantley had been vague. There could have been a misunderstanding about the phone call on Monday. And Rory had provided answers for most of his queries, but . . . Linton collected his thoughts.

'Yes, all right,' he said. 'We'll expect to hear from you, say by Wednesday, and I'll arrange for one of us to meet Derek next Friday.' He stared at Maidment, and there was no mistaking his meaning when he added. 'Please see that the arrangements don't have to be changed this time, Rory. The police are still keen to talk to Derek about that accident, remember, and I shall tell them he's coming.'

No one answered, and as the silence lengthened Linton looked at his watch. He felt defeated, unable to conceive of any other avenues to explore, especially in the presence of this woman, this new complication. He said curtly, 'I think I'd better go. Is it possible to phone for a taxi?'

'My dear Mr Linton, we wouldn't dream of letting you call a cab,' Trina said at once. 'Of course Rory and I will take you to Cointrin. Do you want to leave right now?'

'Yes,' Linton said. 'Thank you.' He avoided meeting his brother-in-law's eye.

Seventeen

While he waited at Cointrin for his London flight Geoffrey Linton tried to phone Peter Bingham at the Berne number Maidment had given him. There was no reply, so he tried the British Embassy. The duty officer was unhelpful, though he eventually and reluctantly admitted that the number Linton had was in fact that of Bingham's home, but that Bingham was away for the weekend; he couldn't – or wouldn't – say where.

Resentful of his wasted Sunday, Linton flew back to Heathrow, collected his car and drove to his Hampstead house. By the time he arrived he was not in the best of tempers, and Julia's reactions to his report irritated him still further.

'I still don't understand why you didn't press Rory harder,' she said at last.

'I've told you. He had a perfectly plausible explanation for everything that's happened.'

'But you weren't really satisfied?'

'Satisfied?' Linton thought for a moment, then made up his mind, 'No, I damn well wasn't!'

'Then why –'

'Oh, for God's sake, Julia. Haven't you been listening? This Carter woman appeared. She seemed to know all about Derek. She said it was all fixed for her to bring him back to the UK next Friday. I could hardly call her a liar, could I?'

'What was she like?'

'English. Attractive. Self-possessed. About thirty. What more do you want to know?'

'And you say she's obviously living with Rory?' Julia sighed. 'He's never mentioned her, and that's unlike Rory. I thought – I hoped – he was going to marry that French girl, Marie-Louise.'

'I haven't the faintest idea what your brother intends to do with any of his women, and frankly at the moment I don't give a damn.' Linton helped himself to a strong whisky and flung himself into an armchair. 'But I'll tell you something: if Derek doesn't arrive on Friday I'm going to raise hell, however embarrassing that may be for everyone.'

'What about Peter Bingham?'

'I'll get hold of him tomorrow. I'll go through the FCO, if necessary.'

Linton was over-optimistic. In spite of a good deal of effort he didn't manage to locate Peter Bingham the next day. All he learnt was that Bingham had gone to Germany for a few days, partly on leave, partly on duty; according to the FCO, no one at the Berne Embassy knew his exact movements, but he was expected back on Tuesday. Against his better judgement, Linton decided to wait. It was just possible, he thought, that Bingham might have decided to take Derek with him.

★

For his part, Peter Bingham had not been idle since Easter Monday. He had kept his word to Maidment but had still instituted discreet inquiries about the likelihood that the terrorist whom Maidment had been compelled to smuggle into Switzerland was in fact Horst Zabel.

Further, since it had been necessary for him to visit Bonn and Berlin on other business towards the end of the week, he had taken the opportunity to make use of his contacts in the BfV – the West German counter-intelligence service which, in the absence of a Federal police force, was responsible for international anti-terrorist operations – to get their views on the matter. He had even persuaded his colleagues in Berlin to put out a few informal feelers in the Democratic Republic.

In a sense, all these inquiries were a salve to Bingham's conscience for not reporting immediately to the authorities the part Maidment had been forced to play. Sooner or later, he knew, he would have to come clean, regardless of young Derek's danger; the stakes were high, and there would probably be international repercussions, if not recriminations. But if he could show that he had spent a useful few days trying to equate Maidment's passenger with Horst Zabel, at least his delay might seem less irresponsible.

Proof, of course, was impossible, but by Sunday evening Bingham was more or less convinced. According to the West Germans the possibility that Zabel – and his associates – had been responsible for the attack on the French President had occurred to them and, though Zabel's recent movements were largely a matter of speculation, nothing that was known was incompatible with such a theory. The BfV were somewhat sceptical about French claims that the would-be assassin was necessarily still in France, but adamant that their own border security had been adequate to prevent his arrival on German soil.

There were many alternatives – Spain or a direct escape to the East, for example – but Switzerland was an obvious choice, for its medical facilities if nothing else. And, though Bingham had no knowledge of Herr Doktor Keller's suicide, by this time he was fully aware that the Director of the Clinique de la Rocque was an eminent plastic surgeon. The inference was obvious, though the details remained obscure.

Bingham decided to return to Berne via Geneva to confront Rory Maidment once again. In any case, he had been out of touch for several days, and there could be fresh news of Derek. On Monday he caught the first flight out of Berlin to Köln, picked up his car, and set off down the Autobahn.

The flight, as so often happened on Berlin routes, had been delayed, and it was a long drive. It was mid-afternoon by the time Bingham arrived in Geneva, and he debated whether to go to the Consulate or straight to Maidment's house. If he went to the office Rory would almost certainly be busy, and might not be too pleased to see him. If he went to the house he could have a wash and make himself comfortable until Rory arrived. He could always phone Rory and suggest he might come home as soon as possible. Bingham plumped for the house.

Stopping only to buy a large Swiss cheese and a bottle of Kirsch as a gift, he drove to the Rue de Haut. As he turned into the courtyard he thought how peaceful the old house looked in the afternoon sun and how happy Rory had often been there with Derek. It seemed unlikely that such pleasant times would come again.

Suddenly depressed, Bingham found the key to the front door, collected his overnight bag and the gifts, and let himself in. He left his bag at the foot of the stairs while he took his purchases along to the kitchen. He felt tired and stiff after his journey, and wondered if it was too early to help himself to a drink. He decided it wasn't.

He was returning to the sitting-room in search of whisky when he heard the noise. He stopped to listen. Footsteps? Someone moving in one of the rooms above? But who would be there? Madame Bichaud didn't come in on Mondays. Rory himself? Derek? It had to be Rory, he thought. He had not been intentionally quiet when he opened the front door and since he had been in the house, but Rory might not have heard him.

Smiling with anticipated pleasure he took the stairs two at a time. 'Hi! Rory! It's me, Peter.'

He flung open the door of the main bedroom, and stopped abruptly. His smile faded as he took in the scene before him. His immediate reaction was embarrassment, and his involuntary instinct was to apologize. 'I – I'm dreadfully sorry,' he stammered.

There were two people in the room, neither of whom

Bingham had ever seen before. The girl, in corduroy slacks and a shirt open to the waist, was standing in the doorway to the bathroom. It was obvious that she had just leapt up from the rumpled bed on which a man in jeans was lying. No wonder they hadn't heard him come into the house, Bingham thought.

He looked from one to the other. The girl, with her high, Slavonic cheekbones, was beautiful. As she leant against the doorpost, she made a picture that appealed to Bingham's artist's eye. But there was a stillness about her, a wariness, like that of an animal ready to pounce.

The man swung his legs off the bed and stood up. He was small – small enough to be a professional jockey – with an expressionless, slightly discoloured face, but nonetheless his personality dominated the room. Almost instinctively Peter Bingham guessed who he was and the reason for the bruising round his eyes and nose. The guess was replaced by certainty as Horst Zabel spoke.

'And who the hell are you, bursting into our bedroom like that?'

The slight American accent was the give-away. It was one of Zabel's attributes that Bingham had learnt of only in the last couple of days. He found himself staring at the little man while thoughts scurried through his mind. So this was the terrorist wanted throughout Europe. The face didn't correspond with the ubiquitous posters, but the reason for that was obvious. The only thing that wasn't clear was what Zabel was doing in Rory Maidment's bedroom – and it really only needed a moment's thought to put two and two together about that aspect of the affair. Bingham knew that a great deal – his life, perhaps – depended on how he played this unexpected scene. He collected his thoughts and replied carefully.

'My name's Bingham, Peter Bingham. I'm a friend of Rory's – a colleague. I have a key to his house. You must be friends of his, too, as you're staying with him.' He paused,